Books by Sharon McAnear

The Jemma Series:

Corner of Blue

In My Bones

Taste of Gold

Dust of Orion

Bless the Moon

Stars in My Crown Trilogy:

Forever a Starry Sky

The Night Hawk

The Peerless Sunshine Queen

Waiting For You Series:

Raining Love in Dove Creek

Raining Love in the Highlands

with Rachel Wells:

Find Me a Man Club

Waiting for You Series

In matters of the heart, patience can be an overrated virtue.
"Keeping the flame burning" gets tiresome after a while.
A bold and weary few snuff it out and take charge...

Waiting for You Series
BOOK ONE

Raining Love in Dove Creek

Sharon McAnear

RAINING LOVE in DOVE CREEK
Copyright © 2016 by Sharon McAnear
Published in the U.S. by: The Torwood Group, Colorado

ISBN-13: 978-1540418531   ISBN-10: 1540418537

Cover design by the Torwood Group
Cover images © Kellie Tate Russell Used by permission
and © Sharon McAnear
Author photo © Sharon McAnear

Raining Love in Dove Creek is a work of fiction. References to real people, events, establishments, organizations, or locales are intended only
to provide a sense of authenticity and are used fictitiously.
All other characters, incidents, and dialogue are drawn from the author's imagination.

Printed in the U.S.A.

For my mother, Margaret Jean Leathers Williams

Acknowledgments

I sincerely appreciate Earlene White, longtime County Clerk of Dolores County, Colorado, and her fine memory and cheerful assistance in my research for this story. Thanks also to my brother, Jan Williams, for helping me find resources and being one himself many times. As always, thanks to my husband, Dwight.

All good things arrive unto them that wait ~
and don't die in the meantime.
~ Mark Twain

Raining Love in Dove Creek

Chapter 1

Room for Rent

*V*iolet Hendricks swung the sledgehammer a final time and the old outhouse crashed apart in splintery pieces. She could have done it methodically, but Violet relished demolishing the most loathsome symbol of her situation. She removed the rusty nails and stacked the boards for kindling. Then she shoveled more dirt into the old pit and raked the topsoil. This time next year, she would be the only one who knew where it used to be. As she spread flower seeds harvested from the front yard into the dirt, her flock of chickens began pecking at them.

"Shoo!" Violet pitched one of her gloves at the biggest hen that flapped away and cackled. The seeds might survive the hens, but if it didn't rain soon, not a one would sprout.

She turned back to survey her new outhouse. Not bad. She had become more proficient every time she had to build one. These boards were from the pigsty behind the barn. She didn't raise pigs any more. Her Papa did when he was in charge. She thought the place stunk bad enough without pigs.

"Who said I need a man?" Violet asked the rooster who was now inspecting the flower seeds as he fertilized the spot. She ran him off and pumped herself a cup of water. She drank her fill and poured the bit that was left into her cat's tin bowl. She didn't *need* a man; she only *wanted* one. And that one and only particular man seemed no longer up for the having.

~

The matchstick poker game had lasted over three hours, and, after mutually agreeing to call it a night, most of the men were heading off to their respective rooms in the grand old boarding house. The place was once a Denver socialite's splendid home, but The Depression had forced the owner to offer parts of it as room and board for members of the Colorado State Senate and House of Representatives. It was only a short walk to the Capitol Building.

State Representative Jenkins Butler, from the large Colorado 58th District, had decidedly won the friendly game, but one of the losers stayed behind to chat with him.

"How do you maintain that stoic face for almost four hours, Jenky?" the Governor asked, puffing on a cigar. "Did it come naturally to you from your dad?"

Jenkins laughed. "Probably. You knew him better than most. Was he any good at poker?"

Governor Ralph Carr patted his young friend on the shoulder. "Your dad made his fortune betting with that poker face of his. Not with poker chips but through investments." He settled on the well-worn leather sofa in the smoky game room. "How are you doing, Jenky? What's your opinion about the goings-on in Europe?"

Jenky blew out his breath. "It looks like all the makings of another war, sir. Hitler must be stopped. He's a maniac."

The Governor put out his cigar. "Seems like just a matter of time before we jump in. I surely hate to see it, but we can't sit in the stands forever. How are things on the Western Slope? I need to get over the mountains and spend more time over there—visit with the farmers and miners, my people. We have a big push coming for getting electric service to those rural areas. Are you ready to get behind the mule and get it done?" He punched Jenky's arm then retrieved his coat from the chair where he'd lost all his matchsticks.

"I certainly am, Governor. You can depend on it. There is nothing I care more about than my constituents."

～

Violet dug her boot heel into the center of a bindweed and twisted hard. Bindweed didn't fool any bean farmer. Yes, it produced small pink and white flowers, but it also spread like butter on a hot cob of corn and choked out young crops. She checked her grandfather's pocket watch then surveyed the horizon. No rain coming today. From her mailbox on the county road, she could see distant mountains in every direction. Most were rooted in her native Colorado, but the others rose from neighboring Utah, Arizona, and New Mexico—the four corners of America. She picked a blue wildflower growing in the borrow ditch and sniffed to see if it was fragrant. Instead she got a big whiff of King's pig farm on the hill northwest of her place.

"Blah." She shook her head like a wet dog and looked heavenward with outstretched hands. "Please send us rain, Lord. Let the wind carry thunderclouds spilling over with moisture rather than the smell of pigs. Amen twice to that."

Her mother, Alice Ann, had called this spot "Kansas with a view", but her dear mother was never happy in rural Dove Creek in her later years. She was a spirited woman who taught at one of the first schools in Dolores County. But towards the end of her life, Alice Ann was often confused and said odd things. Her final words were a stern reminder that she wanted to be buried in Colorado Springs *or else*. Nobody was sure what the threat meant and Nev Hendricks did not have the money to carry his wife almost 400 miles back to the Springs anyway. He died a year after she did in his sleep, and that was almost ten years ago. It was the same year Violet graduated from high school, was first kissed by Jenky Butler a dozen times on a hayride, first read a new cartoon strip about a cute mouse named Mickey, and brought in her first bean crop when everybody in Dolores County said she couldn't do it alone. She kicked at another bindweed. Ten years.

The Hendricks' farm sat in a low, sheltered spot alongside the seasonal Dove Creek. Violet liked that the county road followed the creek and their small house couldn't be seen until rounding that curve. Stately cottonwoods—home to squirrels, songbirds, and crows—framed it perfectly. *A dramatic entrance,* her mother had called it. She had loved drama. The farm wasn't in the mountains, but in the sage-covered hills near the mountains where wheat and bean farmers had cleared millions of sagebrush and rabbitbrush to cultivate crops. Her father had built the house, the barn, all the outbuildings, and had planted the fruit trees. But it was her mother who planted the roses, the honeysuckle bushes, the tulips and columbines, tacked up a trellis for morning glories, made all the curtains, and brought her joyful, spunky spirit to the place. Violet missed them both, dearly.

Now she squinted at Tyrel Fetter's mail truck barreling down the dirt road. A golden-tailed hawk swooped and landed on a fencepost, as if expecting mail. At least if she waited by her mailbox Tyrel would only waste ten minutes of her time. If she stayed out of sight, he would come looking for her and want a cup of coffee. As she swatted at a clump of dirt on her pants' leg, Violet noticed that the twin holes in her overalls were getting bigger. She would have to add more patches to the knees as well as to both elbows of her ancient, plaid shirt. But seeing as how the whole country wasn't quite out of The Great Depression yet, most everybody was skimping and saving to get on with life. Nobody cared that her hand-me-down overalls were falling apart from hard work and old age.

〜

Tyrel brought his Model A pickup to a grating halt, making the dust fly around her. He grinned—or not; his buckteeth made it hard to tell. "How's the Dish of Dove Creek?"

"Gosh, Tyrel. How's your *wife*?" Violet asked, blinking her eyes against the dust. "Did I get any mail?"

He handed her a letter from the bank in Cortez. Her stomach did a flip.

"No parcel post?" she asked, avoiding his watchful eyes.

Tyrel reached into the orange crate in the seat beside him and fished around. "Nope. Got the percolator going?"

She pulled an apologetic face. "Sorry. What's the latest news?"

He gave a shrug. "No coffee—no news." He revved the truck's engine and then grinned. "I'm joking. Let me see…you probably heard about Hollywood starting to film *Gone With The Wind*. Mr. *Twitler* is going nuts, not about Rhett Butler, but about invading Poland. What's with that guy, anyway? Get how I put twit and Hitler together?"

"I get it." She refastened a bobby pin holding back her braid. She'd already heard both those stories at Sitton's General Store.

Tyrel put the truck in gear. "Always joking around, that's me. Gotta make tracks now, missy. I lost time trying to catch that fat hog of King's that was in the road down by the creek. You might keep your eye out for him—the hog, that is. Probably King, too." He glanced at her dilapidated work boots. "Anything special you're looking for in the mail? I reckon it was a pair of high heels like Jean Harlow wears." He snickered through his teeth, and then tried to cover it with a cough.

"Nope, nothing special." Nothing she would tell Tyrel Fetters about.

He leaned out the window with his toothy grin. His beady eyes were mindful of King's grandest hog. "I bet that old house gets lonesome after suppertime. *At your age*, you gotta regret turning down my offer of marriage before the big war."

Violet batted at a fly. "Gosh. I was only a little girl then, Tyrel. Go home to your wife."

He revved the engine again. "Some cultures arrange marriages like that. I read it in the *National Geographic*."

"You mean you read it in Jenky's *National Geographic*. See ya."

His grin faded as the truck clattered off. Violet turned towards her house with the letter that could hold the key to her dream come true.

"At *your* age," she said, mocking Tyrel in her impeccable imitation of cartoon Goofy. He had nerve flirting with her when his wife was slaving away over his kids at home. He was lucky to find that French girl to marry him. Who would want to kiss Tyrel anyway? Now Jenky Butler was another matter. Too bad Jenky was out of her league.

"At your *age*," Violet said again, yanking open the door to the screened-in porch. She let it slam behind her and plopped down on an uneven bench she'd built to use while she took off her boots. One of the frayed laces snapped right in half. She pitched the boot across the room. Her calico cat, Bean, briefly appeared in the kitchen doorway before seeking refuge elsewhere. She pitched the second boot. "*At your age...uh yuck, uh yuck, uh yuck.* What am I supposed to do about it anyway?" Her voice locked up and her eyes glistened, but she wouldn't have it. She sniffed and took the letter to the kitchen table to read. It didn't take long.

April 28, 1939
Dear Miss Hendricks,
We regret that we cannot approve your application for a loan. As you may know, financial times remain fragile and the board must prioritize the more urgent needs of our customers above the luxury requests. Perhaps at some later date we can assist you in your efforts to pipe water into your house. Until that time, it might be wise to consider a savings account with us or buying a U.S. Savings "C" Bond.
Very Truly Yours,
Virgil C. Cates, Loan Officer
Merchant State Bank, Cortez, Colorado

She expected this. Good luck had not found her door in a long while. Violet went to the front room, the *parlor* Papa had called it, and opened his desk drawer. She took out a pin cushion. This was her parents' home, and for the past ten years she had slept in the same bed in which she was born. How sad was that, Tyrel Fetters? She longed to have un-patched sheets and take a real bath in a sparkling white tub, rather than a tin washtub. She daydreamed about not hauling water from the well or not having to heat it on the wood burning stove. She dreaded cutting and chopping wood for the stove in the autumn when she was literally too tired to move.

Violet wanted to use her Sears & Roebuck catalog for ordering—not as toilet paper. Her Sears bath towel would be soft and big and her soap would be from the catalog too, not made from lard in her kitchen. She would step out onto a Sears rose-colored, chenille bath rug, rather than chicken mess as she stepped out of the privy.

Violet stared blankly out the window. There the new one stood in all its glory. She couldn't wait to tear down the wretched thing with a sledge hammer, fill in the pit, plant snapdragons over it, and never build a replacement. It was time for a change, bank or no bank. She would figure out a way. She couldn't depend on anybody but herself.

To the right of Papa's desk she had pinned a calendar from the Merchant State Bank; on either side of it were her "dream" pictures. She pinned the bank letter next to torn-out dream pages from the catalog as a motivator. Featured among the dream pictures was the drawing of the Sears, Roebuck, & Company's *Newcastle*—Modern Home Kit #3402— six rooms and bath, already cut and fitted, with a price tag of $1,631. Next to that was the Newcastle's floor plan, which included the indoor bathroom. Her favorite illustration, though, was from a 1928 catalog, when her folks were still alive. A finely robed gentleman, wearing leather slippers, was shaving in his beautiful bathroom. His profile reminded her of the Honorable Colorado State Representative Edward Jenkins Butler, who only came home to his Dove Creek farm when Colorado's General Assembly was in recess.

Jenky was still single, well-off, and as handsome as he was smart, but he wasn't the valedictorian of their class—she was. But thus far, being lucky in the book brains department had not done her one lick of good. She stood back and sighed.

Violet wilted onto the old loveseat, narrowly missing Bean. He stretched across her legs and she stroked his silky fur. Bean was most likely her best friend. Jenky had a sheepdog named Caesar, but she doubted that he got to practice his herding skills in Denver. Jenky probably also had an elevator and electric lights, as well as a dozen classy girlfriends. She could do with electric lights. Electricity would change everything that bad luck had dumped in her lap.

With electric lights, her Newcastle kit home would shine from top to bottom, day or night, and then she could see how to put on makeup after the sun went down—as though that would do her any good with Jenky living a whole day away. Did he really look like the gentleman in that advertisement when he shaved? She would love to watch him rinse his soapy face and dry it on one of her Sears towels. She lifted Bean off her lap and got her boots on for evening chores. Her having a house with water piped in, lit up with electricity or not, would have to remain a dream, a *castle* in the air.

~

"Just where have you been all my life?" asked the buxom redhead sitting next to handsome Reginald Magee at the roadside diner. Her pink sweater was a little snug but her plaid skirt was full and would twirl well on a dance floor.

Dressed in chinos, a white shirt, and a checkered vest, Reg pointed his last French fry at her. "I was about to ask you the same thing, girly-girl."

"You first," she said, raising a shoulder as she fluttered her lashes at him like Minnie Mouse.

He wiped his lips with a paper napkin, wadded it up, and dropped it onto his empty plate, looking into her eyes the whole time. "You are such a natural beauty. Have you ever been photographed by a professional?"

She smiled, showing a slight gap in her front teeth, right behind her pouty red lips. "I have not, but I bet you say that to all the girls you meet."

Reg moved close to her. "Now, that's a bet you would lose. How about you finish up that milkshake and let's fly this coop."

"All done here, sir." She grinned as she pushed the half-full glass back.

He laid a quarter on the counter and offered his arm to the giggling young lady.

They walked to his convertible. She ran her hand over the seats. "Ooh. swell car. You really are a big shot photographer and have dreamy green eyes."

"That's me all right." Reg opened the passenger door and she slid in. Propping his elbows on the doorframe, he surveyed this sweet creature and gave her a wink. "Let's go for a spin. Any place in particular?"

She considered choices. "Lookout Point. Nobody goes there in the daytime. Are you really going to take pictures of me?"

"Of course. Say, what's the name of this town, anyway?" he asked as he lit a cigarette and started the car.

She scooted closer to him. "Walsenburg, Colorado. Where are you headed?" Her fingers were already in his curly blond hair. "Turn right at the next street."

The convertible's tires squealed a little as he took the corner. "I have a big assignment in the Four Corners area." He pitched out his cigarette and eased his arm around her. "What's your name, Sweet Cheeks?"

"Agnes." She snuggled against him. "Are you nervous?"

"About my assignment? Nah. This is not my first time to take on an exciting project."

"Well, it's my first time." She looked up at him with big cow eyes.

"Is that so? How old are you, Agnes?"

"Twenty-one." Her voice went up at the end, as in a question.

He pulled the car over under an elm tree. "Let me give you a lift home, Agnes. I should be getting on the road. Honest."

"But what about the photos? You said you would." She folded her arms and moved away.

"I'll be back through this way after my assignment is finished. I'll look you up. What's your last name?"

She sniffed. "Faraday."

Reg's brow bunched up. "As in *Re-elect Faraday for Sheriff*, like on all the billboards?"

"That's my daddy." She blew her nose into the handkerchief he'd provided.

Reg gunned the engine and made a U-turn.

"This is not the way to my house."

"I'll take you back to the diner and you can get home from there." He lit another cigarette.

"You smoke too much. I bet your kisses taste like a rotten potato smells."

Reg pulled in front of the diner. "You take care, Agnes. Hope your dad wins the election."

She slammed the door and straightened her hair. "Look what your silly convertible has done to me."

He waved and grinned as he got back on the main road. "Whew. Close call, Reggie, old boy. Now let's see if we can find some music in the hinterlands." He turned on his car radio and sailed towards the first mountain range on his journey.

~

After the evening chores were done, Violet sat on the front porch and ate her homemade bread and peach preserve sandwich, along with a Coca-Cola she'd been saving in the ice box. The honeysuckle vine was about to burst into bloom, then the hummingbirds would come. Nothing like a honeysuckle blossom to turn her thoughts to her handsome neighbor. She watched a trio of deer make their way down the hillside and then disappear into the piñon trees next to the barn. Most likely, they were headed to the creek that separated her bean field from one of Jenky's. The town of Dove Creek got its name from that creek. Her father had transplanted baby ponderosa pines where his land met the Butler's and the trees were taller than the barn now. The Hendricks and Butler families enjoyed many Sunday picnics at their pine stand.

She took the last bite of her sandwich but swallowed it whole as the Honorable Edward Jenkins Butler's shiny blue pickup drove past. *He was home for the summer.* Her heart fluttered and she took a breath. Nothing would come of it. Settle into your spinsterhood, Violet. Just break even with this year's crop. Deep breath. *Oh, Jenky.*

The pinto beans had been in the earth for over three weeks, waiting for the first spring rain and the chance of more to follow. The skies remained a clear, crisp blue. Her detective comic book ordered from a used bookstore in Denver would arrive soon. If not, she could spend more wishful evenings with Bean and her already earmarked, 1939 Spring Edition of the Sears catalog. Edward Jenkins Butler, youngest member of the Colorado House of Representatives, had popped up right on time to torture her dreams again. How long could she continue like this? There were too many dry years between those perfect kisses in 1929 and his dutiful hugs each summer at church or at Sitton's store. He had other plans, other commitments to the good people of his district. Nuts to that.

Regardless of the lonesomeness of her evenings spent by the kerosene lamp, the solitude offered her plenty of time to pray for rain and to come up with notions for earning extra money. She had a few already. Only the good Lord could come up with the rain.

Two days later, Violet went into Dove Creek. Her little hometown was situated where the main road from Cortez, Colorado, to Monticello, Utah, angles sharply to the west. Years ago, Violet had often attended sledding parties at a friend's house at the top of a hill in town. Back then, she had thought the hill was a mountain. Actually, the area was a mixture of level spots and gentle hills. Sagebrush, piñon trees, and elms dotted its landscape. Old cottonwoods kept company with the creek, but the town was surrounded by perfect land for bean and wheat farming and then there were also those terrific mountain views. It was a good place to grow up.

She drove past the grain elevators, post office, assay office, half a dozen churches, the Grange Hall, the movie theater, and the drug store, then parked in the shade of an elm tree near Sitton's General Store. She walked on the hard-packed dirt that served as a sidewalk up to the long porch. It was her plan to tack the note on the General Store's bulletin board without being noticed, but the white-haired, plump Ethel Sitton didn't miss much.

"How are you doing, young lady?" Mrs. Sitton said as she slipped her arm around Violet's waist. "Goodness, but you don't have an ounce of extra meat on your bones." Ethel and her husband, Howard, owned Sitton's General Store. She tended to the food, clothing, and home necessities side while Howard, white-haired and stooped but still sharp as a tack, ran the other side—hardware, feed, and seed. He also sat around shooting the breeze with other old timers. Their kids were grown and moved away to the busy front range of the Rockies, rather than raise beans on the rural western slope.

"I'm all right, Ethel. Hope it rains soon." She was prepared for the lecture she got with each turn of a new season from this kindly, well-intentioned lady.

Mrs. Sitton trained her bifocals on her. "I think about you all alone in that house, dear. You should come to more dances and socials at the Grange Hall or at least get yourself to church more often. Have fun. Meet folks. We're having a box supper in two weeks. There's a new high school teacher in town. He's a bachelor." She dusted cat hair off Violet's shirt. "You were such a beauty as a girl, but goodness knows, you've let yourself go to pot. And all for that farm. What would your dear, dainty mother say? God rest her. You have the same deep blue eyes and wavy, dark hair as she did." She tapped her finger on the strap fastener of Violet's big overalls. I do recall that you wore lipstick in high school and Alice Ann always sewed your dresses in the latest fashion, even if the fabric was feed sacks. Some of the patterns were colorful."

"Sorry to disappoint you, Ethel. I'm way too busy and tired to socialize, but I appreciate the concern." That wasn't exactly the truth, but it was good manners.

Mrs. Sitton led her to the ladies wear display and whispered, "You pick out anything and I'll let you have it for practically pennies. It's time you wore something besides your father's work clothes or you're never gonna catch a husband. Look at those shoes. Why, you need laces, dear. Come with me."

"I need to get to the ice house and back before noon or my food's going to spoil." Mrs. Sitton wasn't listening. Violet followed behind, but glanced back at her note:

ROOM FOR RENT Inquire at Hendricks Farm

~

Violet chipped away at the ice block with a pick until it would fit perfectly into the compartment of her Crystal Ice Box. The second block was still wrapped in gunny sacks and waiting its turn to be placed in a large crock in the cellar. She emptied the drip tray underneath the ice box and replaced it. Now, if she chipped off one more sliver from the block, she could cool a glass of fresh milk to drink with her lunch.

Someone knocked on the front door. That was quick. Her note had only been posted a few hours ago and already she had a nibble. She should take a peek and see if it was a hobo or a hairbrush salesman. Neither of those prospects would do.

The man at the door was taller than her own five feet and nine inches, and was wearing a nice-looking suit. She couldn't see his face because he had his back to her. She checked her bobby pins, pinched her cheeks for color, and opened the door.

The man turned around with a big smile. "Hello, sweet Vi." His voice was a rich baritone.

Her breath caught in her throat. "Jenky!"

He held out his arms. "You were wearing those exact clothes the last time I saw you. It's good to be consistent." His face was fuller than last summer, but he still had those good Butler jaw lines. And she couldn't take her eyes off his perfect lips, she knew how good his long-ago kisses were.

Violet blushed and let him hug her for a second time. That's when she noticed she still had the ice pick in her hand. "Sorry. If I'd known a Representative would be paying me a social call, I would have bought some new overalls."

He studied her face. "How are you, Vi?"

"Uh...really well." She smiled and clasped her hands behind her so he wouldn't see the ice pick or notice the holes in her shirt. There wasn't much she could do to hide the holes in her britches. Jenky smelled good, like limeade. His eyes were still the color of milk chocolate and his hair was as black as the night.

"Are you going to invite me in?" he asked.

"Oh...sure. Come in," Violet said, walking backwards in the opposite direction of the front door.

"What do you have that you don't want me to see?" Jenky asked, trying to take a look.

"Nothing. Don't be so nosy."

Jenky stepped inside and surveyed the old-style parlor. "And it's exactly like it was ten years ago in here. You haven't become a hermit, have you, Vi? Do you ever open the curtains?"

She covertly laid the ice pick on a lamp table. "Did you come to insult me?"

He laughed and held out a slender packet wrapped in brown paper. "Actually, I am delivering your mail. It was left in my box yesterday by mistake."

Violet turned red at the thought of him accidentally opening her detective comic book. She quickly took the packet and eased it on top of the ice pick. "Thank you. Tyrel is a bonehead."

"Don't be too hard on him. He could have had some rough combat service in France."

"He was a mail clerk in the war and he reads your National Geographic before you get it."

"I know. Do I smell coffee brewing?"

A smile eased its way across her face. "I'll see if I can rustle up some. I have leftover biscuits, too." Her heart was doing cartwheels.

Jenky Butler was easy to talk to unless he got into a debate. But that was what he and Violet did best in high school. Argue. He loved playing the Devil's Advocate.

"What was that boy's name who wet his pants on stage during our school play?" she asked.

"Poor guy. He was so nervous. That was Teddy Baker."

"No." She shook her head. "It wasn't Teddy Baker. The Bakers moved right before we started rehearsing." Violet knew she was right.

"I don't think so. It was the Baker boy. Remember we used to tease him about needing his Teddy bear so he wouldn't cry during algebra?"

"That was Teddy Shoals. He was the clumsy guy who fell into the creek and got into trouble for tracking mud into the classroom. Mr. Gleason slipped on it and made Teddy stay after school to clean it up by hand. It was not Teddy Shoals either."

"Oh, yeah." Jenky casually brushed biscuit crumbs off his shirt and put them in his coffee cup. He snapped his fingers. "It was Flynn Evans.

Big guy. Always wore overalls. He was a wreck when the curtain opened."

"I always wear overalls." Violet's brow lifted. "You said so yourself."

His ears reddened. "You make overalls look better than Flynn did, though."

"Well, it wouldn't have been so bad if it hadn't been our senior year and if we weren't doing Shakespeare. Wonder what Mr. Gleason was thinking."

"At least it was a Dove Creek version of Shakespeare. I doubt The Bard would have recognized his work."

They smiled at the memories and at the tenderness in one another's eyes. Violet thought he was about to reach for her hand, but he picked up the butter knife instead and then laid it back on the table.

"Remember when the Swenson twins had us over to ride in that bucket on a rope from the windmill tower to their tree house?" he asked.

"How could I forget that," Violet said with a giggle. "They hid a garter snake in the bucket when it was my turn. I screamed so loud that Mr. Swenson came in from the field to see what had happened."

They both laughed. She could tell that he was considering taking a risk in the conversation. His ears were bright red.

"How about the hayride the summer after graduation? Any good memories there?" Jenky asked quietly without making eye contact.

She nodded, not mentioning anything specific.

"You ever wear your hair unbraided, like you did that night?"

"No. It gets in my way. I might let it down for a special reason or something," she said, "but one hasn't presented itself."

He shifted around in his chair. Then the only sound for a long stretch was that of hens clucking in the chicken yard. She glanced at Jenky to see if by some miracle he might want to repeat the events of the hayride. She was ready to kiss the dickens out of him.

"I see you are still driving your dad's old Maxwell," he said instead.

Violet chugged down what was left of her coffee. "I spend a lot of my time under the hood though." She began clearing the table.

"Time for a new car then," Jenky said, momentarily distracted by Bean jumping on his lap.

"It may be time, but some of us can't afford to buy a new car. I have the Farmall your dad gave me, but I have to keep it running, too. It has seen better days. Shoo, Bean."

Jenky stroked the cat. "He's okay, aren't you buddy?" Bean purred and closed his eyes. "I could loan you the money, Vi. You need a dependable car. My truck purrs along like a bright blue cat or I would trade it in."

"I suppose you have electricity and running water, too," Violet said, then thought better of it. She knew the Butler home was the first in the area to have plumbing, but nobody had power unless you had a business. "I meant living in metropolitan Denver, that is."

He kept his eyes on the cat. "I also have a telephone in Denver. One at my apartment and another in my office. Do you hold that against me?"

"I don't hold anything against you," she said, now also watching Bean.

"Then why don't you answer my letters?"

"You mean those letters that begin with *Dear Constituent…?*"

Jenky drew back. "No, I mean my letters to you, personally."

"I never got any personal letters. When did you ever write to me?" Violet pitched the dish rag onto the counter and stood with her damp hands on her hips.

"In college, in law school, and every year since. Once a year at Christmas," he said with a straight face. "I would have written much more often if you had responded."

Violet's eyes went big. "What? You're talking about Christmas cards. People don't answer Christmas cards, Jenky Butler. I think you have lost your common sense in the big city."

"Why not?" He still held a straight face. "How else was I supposed to keep in touch, if I were so inclined?"

"If you were so inclined?" Violet had held her feelings in for a long time on this issue. "We should have been more than neighbors, Jenky, but it never happened. We kissed like crazy on a hayride and then *poof* that was that. Did I scare you or are you the most timid man in history? For all I know, you had a girl in college or in law school or in Denver right now. Has it ever occurred to you to come to see me, *if you were so inclined*? Wait." She went to the kitchen window. "I don't see your precious pickup out there, so you must have walked the whole way just to bring my mail. I seem to recall that you and I once made a secret path between our houses and swore that we would never let it grow over. There is barely anything left of it now. What does that say about us?"

He grimaced. "I didn't know if you wanted my company since you didn't answer my letters."

She looked heavenward for patience. "They weren't letters, Jenky, but I still have all of them if that means anything to you."

He seemed genuinely confused. "Then why did you keep them if they weren't real letters?"

Violet paused, but then busied herself putting away the leftover jam and pouring water to rinse their cups. She wanted to tell him that she kept them because he might have licked the envelopes and the stamps, and because his hand must have moved across the cards when he signed them, but instead she blurted out…"You have no idea. You never have. After that hayride you should have been on our doorstep the next morning and every morning after that until you went to work in Denver for the summer. Furthermore, a letter to me should begin with…*Dear Violet. How are you*? I figured you were sending Christmas cards to all of your constituents."

"I wasn't. I only mailed the one to you." Jenky scraped his chair against the wooden floor and stood. Bean scampered from the room. "You're too hard to please, Vi. I had forgotten that. And you *are* close to becoming a hermit. Look at yourself."

They were standing very near to one another. She only looked him in the eye once, but his gaze never veered. She didn't know if it was his heartbeat or her own that filled her ears.

"Thanks for the coffee and biscuits. I'm working to get REA into the Southwest faster so you can have what I have in Denver."

Her mouth was dry. "Your constituency appreciates the effort."

He stared at the floor. "Don't take in a boarder, Vi. I can loan you money for whatever you need."

She sucked in her lips. "Oh. Money is what this visit is about."

"I saw your note on Sitton's board. It's too risky to have a stranger in the house. Your papa would not like this at all."

Violet scowled at him as her words pounced. "My papa is gone. Your dad is gone. Our mothers are gone. It's you and me now. You have five times as much land as I do. You went to college and law school. I didn't. You have an important job in a big city. I raise beans and I was born in that bedroom back there where I still sleep. I will soon be twenty-eight years old and I have to make my own future. I need money to pipe water into my house whether anybody likes it or not. I want to live in the modern world. I know The Depression hit everybody, but you seem to have come through it with no problem."

Jenky nodded, calmly. "Like I said, I will loan you the money, Violet, without interest. I don't care how you use it. Buy that house from Sears I can see you've pinned to the wall. I'll help you set it up, but don't take in a boarder. This house isn't made to turn into a boarding house. You're too… young…and…healthy to be a landlady. I'm thinking of your reputation."

"That Sears house is none of your business. For your information, I've fixed up the tack room in the barn. I put the spare bed out there and some other things. It will be fine for the summer. I don't intend to run a boarding house and my reputation is probably that of an old maid." She was sweating. "Thank you for the loan offer."

He started to the door. "So, you hold my good fortune against me. It was my intention to…" He looked away. "I have worked hard for it, Vi."

Bean rubbed against her trembling legs. "I know. But there's your kind of hard work and there's my kind of hard work. You are a self-made success and I am a self-made hermit. It's the way life is."

Jenky cut his eyes at her. "No hard feelings meant with that comment. I…we may have missed out on certain opportunities along the way, but I do admire what you've done by yourself. I can't say that I admire what you've done *to* yourself. Don't go sour on the world, Vi." He exhaled. "Good luck with your boarder, then. Take care."

He pushed on the screen and left.

Violet rushed to the door and shouted. "Thanks for bringing my mail."

He raised his hand and kept walking.

Shoot. Shoot. Shoot.

~

Violet sat on the porch for an hour, thinking he might return and sweep her up in his arms. She even walked along their secret trail to see if he could have a romantic compulsion to do the same thing and they would greet one another with passionate kisses. Nope. Jenky was obviously at home, and perhaps marking her off his brief Christmas card list.

She fed Bean but skipped her own meal. He had said she was becoming a hermit and he didn't admire what she was doing to herself. *Sour on the world.* She bet he made that up on the spot and was actually about to say that she was turning into a hag. Violet stood sock-footed in front of her grandma's pedestal mirror. She normally used it only to drape her shirts over. The mirror had tiny black spots all over it and a small crack at the bottom, but she could at least check and see what all the fuss was about her appearance.

There she stood as her true self—a hardworking farmer. She was already aware that her work boots were pathetic, but she wasn't going to waste money on a new pair. The saddle soap that she found when she cleaned out the tack room would help. Okay then; so what if both pairs of her overalls were patched? She washed them once a week and they still had some good wear left.

The dark dress she wore to funerals (and would most likely wear to her own) was hanging in the musty wardrobe, as was her mother's dark purple duster that Violet wore over the dress to church. There was a pair of lace-up, oxford shoes in there, too. She owned two shirts and both were red and black plaid. With her single braid hanging past her shoulders, she did lack any appealing feminine qualities, and it was true that her mother had, out of necessity, dressed her like a feed sack princess as a girl. True also, that she wore lipstick in high school. It was still in the top dresser drawer if she felt like wearing it while she drove the tractor or milked the cow. She giggled.

It was too late for her to catch a man anyway. The only one she wanted was married to his job. It was possible Jenky had a fancy someone in Denver. Perhaps she was his secretary, the one who sent out all those *Dear Constituent* letters. His full name signature on the Christmas cards was his own writing, though. She knew every little loop and dot. Dang it. He smelled so good and called her *sweet* Vi, like he did in high school.

Violet lit the lamp next to her bed and crawled between the sheets with the packet Jenky had brought. She unwrapped it carefully. There was a receipt and a note about the detective comics changing its name and this issue would introduce a new character by the name of Superman. Violet snuggled down with the comic book featuring a hero with midnight black hair, like Jenky's.

Chapter 2

Reginald Magee

*T*hree days later, Violet was changing the oil in her black Maxwell when she heard a shout. She walked around to the front of the house and found a tall man with curly blond hair on her porch. His smile was wide and his clothes were not from around Dove Creek. He had the look of an adventurer on safari, but without a pith helmet, and he was as good looking as he could get—to still be on her porch and not in Hollywood. She wiped her hands on her overalls.

He took off his brown newsboy cap. "Hello, sir. I'm looking for a Mr. Hendricks. Is that you?"

Violet laughed. Surely she didn't look that bad. "I'm *Miss* Hendricks. There is no Mr. Hendricks. Are you here about the room?"

The fellow was obviously embarrassed. "I'm a dunce, ma'am. Of course you aren't a man. I'll have to get my eyes tested. Yes, I'm here to inquire about the room." He hustled over to her and extended his hand. "I'm Reginald Magee. I saw the note at the general store in town. The shopkeeper gave me directions."

I bet Mr. Sitton hated that. Violet shook hands with Reginald. He didn't have a firm grasp, but his eyes were such a perfect shade of green. "What brings you to Dove Creek, Mr. Magee?"

"Just call me Reggie or Reg. I'm a photographer on assignment for *National Geographic*. We are looking at rural Western America as the Depression comes to a close. That kind of thing." He was a fast talker.

"Where are you from?" she asked.

"I'm a New Yorker, but my work takes me all over. How much for the room?"

"Wouldn't you like to see it first?" she asked. "It's not in the house. I fixed up the tack room next to the barn." She wiped her hands on her overalls again and started for the barn.

"The barn?" His grin faded. "You mean without running water or electricity?"

Violet laughed. "There's neither of those in the house either. No farmers have that. I do have a windmill that pumps water from a well, hand-dug by my father, and there's a kerosene lamp and a camp heater in the room. How long are you expecting to be in this area?"

"For the summer," he said, eyeing the outhouse.

Slow down, heart. The tack room was accessed through a side door. She held it open for him and kept it that way.

He stepped inside. "This isn't too bad. It's closed off from the animals and has a window."

"I like it out here." Violet pulled back the feed sack curtains. "It still smells like leather. My papa made saddles at night, but I had to sell most of them during The Depression to make ends meet." She moved to a single saddle in the corner. "I kept this one. It belonged to my grandpa who died from influenza in 1918. He was a master saddle maker." Violet ran her hands over it.

Reg watched her closely. She was unaware of his attention.

"I did my homework out here sometimes when I was a little girl." Violet smiled at the memory. "Oh, I didn't mention that the rent includes two meals a day and all the water you can carry for yourself."

Reg looked around the small area. It was not much more than a bed with linens, a pitcher and bowl, a straight-back chair next to a spindly table with a kerosene lamp, a coat rack, and a kerosene heater .

"Are you a great cook?" he asked.

"I like my cooking. I'm asking ten dollars a month, cash, in advance. Plus no liquor on my property."

"Did the news about repealing prohibition not make it to Dove Creek yet?"

"It's my place and my rules."

"When do the meals start?" Reg asked.

"As soon as I have the ten dollars."

He opened his wallet and took out ten bills. A sudden blast of wind blew the money around and into the barnyard. They laughed as they retrieved it.

"Where do you get your news? I like to keep an eye on the world."

Violet counted the money and put it in the front pocket of her overalls. She snapped it closed. "There's a radio at Sitton's store and they post the day's headline stories on their bulletin board."

"Aces," Reg said as they walked towards the house.

"What do you mean *aces*? There's the outhouse, by the way," Violet said, pointing at the ugliest thing on her farm.

"Thanks. *Aces* is slang, as in 'terrific' or 'that's the spirit."

Violet nodded. "It's your byword. You get set up in the tack room and I'll make lunch. You can pull your car around by the barn if you want.

Park it in the shade of the trees. What kind of car is that anyway?"

Reg grinned. "It's a Ford Roadster convertible. Do you like it?"

The color of it was the same warm brown as Jenky's eyes. "Don't see many convertibles around here. I like the red wheels." Violet grinned and went inside the house.

~

They were finished with the tomato soup and buttered bread lunch, but were still at the table. Reg was entertaining Violet with his funny stories about constantly being on the road. There was a knock at the front door.

"Excuse me." Violet went to the door and opened it without peeking out. It was Jenky.

He smiled at her. "I'm here with a peace offering." He held out a large bundle wrapped in Sitton's familiar brown butcher paper. "May I come in?"

Violet couldn't think straight. She took the bundle from him and set it in the rocking chair.

"Everything okay out there, kiddo?" Reg asked from the kitchen.

Violet and Jenky stared at one another. Her face told the story. Jenky stepped into the kitchen at the same moment Reg stood, wiping his chin on the back of his hand.

Jenky remained calm, probably due to his political background. He shook hands with Reg.

"Jenkins Butler," he said, noticing the remains of lunch. "I'm a longtime friend of Violet's. I live just over the hill."

Reg shifted his eyes knowingly at Violet. "Reginald Magee. I'm her new tenant."

Jenky folded his arms. "What's your business in our area, Mr. Magee?"

"Freelance photography. On a couple of assignments with *National Geographic Society*," Reg said rather pompously.

"What's the subject matter?" Jenky said, becoming even more perturbed at such a romantic job. Bean sat at his feet, observing Reg as well.

Violet was still in the doorway. "The effect of the Great Depression on us poor farmers in the West. You can leave now, Jenky."

Reg grinned at the scene he had obviously instigated.

Jenky looked Reg over. "I live just over the hill, less than a mile away."

"So you said." Reg smirked. "I'll sure keep that in mind if something comes up we can't handle."

"See that you do," Jenky said and lingered a moment before turning to Violet. "Sorry to have interrupted your lunch, Vi. I'll be checking on you." He let himself out the back door with Bean right behind him.

Violet called for Bean but with no results. She heard Jenky's pickup start up and leave.

"Is Mr. Butler your boyfriend?" Reg asked, intrigued.

"No," she said a little too emphatically. "I guess he was in high school, but that's water down the creek now."

"Aha. It's a one-sided affair. Those die hard. Thanks for the lunch. It was tasty. I should get going. I need to make some telephone calls. Where's the nearest phone?"

Violet turned to him. "What's that?"

"A telephone. You know, like in the movies."

"Of course. Sorry. Sitton's store has one."

He put a damper on his amusing observations. "Then I'm off. You need anything?"

"No thanks. Watch out for the crazy mailman. He drives in the middle of the road."

"Will do," Reg said and left, chuckling to himself about his clever phone comment. He put on his newsboy cap.

~

Bean jumped onto the bundle Jenky had brought and gave it a good sniffing while Violet cleaned the kitchen. He made himself comfortable on top of it until she shooed him away.

She untied the string and moved back the paper to discover the contents: two pairs of overalls, a sturdy blue shirt with yellow flowers on it, a similar gray shirt trimmed with red and purple flowers, and a new pair of work boots. A note inside explained: *I am proud of you.*

Violet sat in the rocker to make sense of it all. She forgot herself for a minute and cried. Bean slipped into the kitchen and curled up in his basket.

~

She got nothing but the essentials accomplished over the next few days. When she wasn't cooking, she was stewing about what to cook.

"Different shirt. I like it," Reg said at dinner on Friday.

Violet avoided his eyes. "Thank you."

"The chicken and dumplings was first-rate."

"Was it aces?"

"You got it, kiddo. I saw a notice about a box supper and dance at the Grange Hall this weekend. We should go."

"There would be mass hysteria. I never go anywhere but to church, the ice house in Cahone, the General Store, the bean elevator, and sometimes into Cortez."

Reg tipped his chair back. "Well, it's time you did. I need local photos and a local escort would be advantageous. You'll be doing me a favor."

"How would you repay me?" She meant it to be a joke, like he could carry in wood for her.

He leaned over and kissed her forehead. "There. Paid in advance, like my rent."

Violet dropped her fork. "I was kidding. Gosh, you must think I'm a floozy."

He laughed. "Not in those overalls. You be thinking about what you'll cook for your box supper. I'll be counting my money to bid on it." He pulled on his cap. "I'm talking with people as they come to the ice house today in Cahone. I'll bring us back a block or two."

"That would be aces. Thanks." She giggled and waved at him through the screen. It was comforting the way he tossed "we" and "us" into their many conversations, but the kiss was shocking. They didn't know each other that well yet. New Yorkers must kiss more freely than Dove Creekers.

When word got around to Jenky, he would raise a stink about her being out and about with Reggie if she went to the Grange Hall for the box social. He wouldn't be the only one, either. It might not look proper for a landlady to be socializing with her renter. Those same folks had said it wasn't proper for her to be running a bean farm all alone and it would never work. That was part of the reason she had done it—to prove them wrong. Anyway, Jenky could take a few lessons from Reg about how to have fun more often than every ten years.

Still, Violet wasn't so sure about this particular event. What if Reggie wasn't the high bidder on her box and she wound up having to eat with the epitome of body odor, Snyder Skaggs, or creepy old man Archer? But she could make her mother's special cake that was famously delicious and share it with Reg. What if Jenky was at the event? He often attended local gatherings to discuss politics with his blessed constituency. Let him be there. She had already sent him a cautiously worded thank you note in the mail for the new clothes. She had to admit that the gesture and the note were very sweet of him.

Violet had the chores done and her box supper ready to go. She spent the afternoon pasting tin foil stars all over a lidded cardboard box that she found behind Sitton's. She sat on the porch steps waiting for Reggie. He had come home late after driving up McElmo Canyon near Cortez to photograph small farms and the farmers living there. She heard his car start, and then he backed it up to the steps. Bing Crosby was singing on his radio.

"Need more time?" he asked.

"No. I'm ready."

He chuckled. "You're kidding me. This is a social, not a barn-raising."

"What are you talking about?"

"You have to doll up. Put on a dress and your dancing shoes." He turned the car off and got out. "I'll take care of this," he said, taking the box. "Change out of those overalls." He winked.

Violet froze. She couldn't remember when a man under fifty had winked at her, except in when they played the "Winkum" game at parties.

"Okay," she said as though she had a wardrobe full of suitable frocks. A few minutes later she returned wearing her black dress and black oxfords.

Reg whistled. "That's more like it." He had the top down on the car. "Good thing your hair is pulled back because we are going to see what this little baby can do when mama and papa are running late."

Violet gulped and clung to the box in her lap. She hoped her stars didn't blow off, but she took pleasure in the fact that he included her in the "mama" reference.

The Grange Hall was one of the buildings in Dove Creek that had power. The lights were blazing as they drove up. Violet cringed when she saw Jenky's pickup. Reg gathered his photography equipment while she managed the box and got out by herself.

"I was coming to help. You are lovely in your social garb."

Violet exhaled. "I only wear this to funerals. Everybody is going to notice that I'm not wearing my overalls and wonder who died."

"Nobody will notice any such thing. It's all in your head." Reg offered his arm, but she was afraid she might drop the box in the process. They made their way up the steps and heard bids being yelled out for the first box. Cigarette smoke glazed the air. Reg whispered that he needed to get busy and he would catch up with her later.

~

Violet felt dozens of eyes surveying her funeral dress as she set her box on the long table with the others. Social Chairwoman, Nell Haggerty, with her mass of gray hair piled high and her small mouth boosted with a glob of red lipstick, nodded her approval of the box and scowled slightly at the funeral dress as she wrote a number on the tardy, but star-studded entry. Her husband, Dale, was the auctioneer. Violet retreated into the crowd. As soon as she did, she sensed a familiar presence.

"Who died?" Tyrel Fetters asked, and then snorted so near her ear that a drop of spittle escaped through his buckteeth and landed on her cheek. So much for Reg's theory. Violet pretended not to notice Tyrel and moved to the other side of the room. To add to her anxiety, she wound up right behind Jenky and a pack of his staunchest supporters who seemed oblivious to the auction. She might call more attention to herself if she moved again.

Reggie, meanwhile, snapped photos, moving among the attendees like a sheep dog not missing a twitch within his herd. Violet watched as box after box went for thirty-five, forty, and fifty-five cents—tops. Hers was next.

"Now we come to our final entry, ladies and gentleman. Inside this starry box we have a delicious supper prepared by the prettiest bean farmer in Dolores County. Violet Hendricks, please stand up while we see who gets to share this fine meal with you.

Everyone shuffled around to see where she was. Could the night get any worse? She clutched her skirt and forced herself up from the chair and right back down. It was long enough for Jenky to notice though, before the bidding began.

"Who'll give me fifty cents for this box?" Dale asked. Snyder Skaggs raised his hand. Everyone around him leaned away from the underarm odor.

Oh, please let there be someone else. Laudell Archer, the ickiest old bachelor in the Four Corners area, blurted out "Fifty-one", then jiggled his eyebrows at Violet. From the back of the room, she heard a shout of "Seventy-five cents". She turned around and saw Reggie, who had halted his picture-taking to participate. There was hope.

She jumped when Jenky used his politician voice and said, "Five dollars."

A murmur trickled through the crowd.

"Five dollars and a nickel," Reg responded meekly.

"Ten dollars," Jenky said without hesitation.

The crowd swiveled around to see what Reg would do. He was already back to taking pictures. They all looked toward Dale to proclaim a winner.

"Going once…going twice…sold…to the Honorable Jenkins Butler for an unprecedented ten bucks! Enjoy your meal, Jenky." Dale delivered the box himself to the winner. He grinned at Violet who tried to disappear into the chair.

The crowd applauded, whistled, and then everyone folded up his chair, claimed his box and found his supper mate. Jenky's group dispersed and the two of them were alone in their folding chairs, one behind the other.

"Should I take this home to eat it or would you care to join me?" he asked over his shoulder.

"Suit yourself." Not what she meant to say. "That was embarrassing."

Jenky, wearing his Sunday slacks and button-up vest and tie, brought the box and sat beside her. "It's for a worthy cause. Are you against worthy causes, too?"

"I hardly think that the Grange's Fourth of July parade float fund is a true worthy cause." Violet sniffed. "Was that your way of saying I am against you, personally? You got my vote in the election."

He lowered his voice. "I'm not running for anything tonight. I would like to have a pleasant conversation with you and eat this expensive meal in your company." He looked her over. "Only you could make that dress look stunning, Vi."

"Gosh, Jenky. Have you become a fashion critic? Would you rather that I wore overalls? You said I was hard to please, how about yourself?" She stood so quickly that her chair fell to the floor.

Reggie appeared, unnoticed, and set it up for her. "How's that supper coming? Looks like you two are the last ones to dive in."

Jenky glared at him and offered his arm to Violet. "We are fine. Come on, Vi, let's sit by the stage."

Reg flashed a grin. "Something sure was smelling good all the way over here. You haven't taken the lid off yet. Save some of that cake for me, kiddo."

Jenky steered her away and Violet shrugged at Reg.

Violet wasn't hungry. She watched Jenky eat the meatloaf, potato cakes, and pinto beans without saying a word. He took particular care in devouring every crumb of the cake. He dabbed at his mouth with a napkin and set the box on the floor.

"Once again, I apologize for my comments. You are always lovely, no matter what you wear."

Violet squirmed in her chair, glancing at him a few times. "I was wearing the new clothes you gave me and the shoes too, but Reg suggested I dress up for this high society social event."

Jenky looked around for Reg like a hungry coyote. "So he's the one up on the latest fashion? What nerve to swoop in here and boss you around." His face colored up. "What gives him that right? You wouldn't have done it if *I* had suggested that you change clothes. You would have been offended and picked a fight with me."

She stopped fidgeting. "You have tried to boss me around all our lives. I need a fresh opinion. I can't wait on you forever, Jenkins. Besides, I make my own final decisions."

He was lost in thought. "Do you have locks on your door? I'll come by and take care of that."

Violet wagged her finger at him. "Hold it right there. If I want locks on my doors, I am capable of buying and installing them. I have a screwdriver that works. It's not like Reg is a drifter. He is a professional photographer for *National Geographic*. For Pete's sake, he just finished a series on Mesa Verde." She sighed. "Gosh, Jenky, nobody else is worried about this except you."

"Oh, they are worried all right. They come to me with their concerns. Even photographers know a gorgeous girl when they see one."

Butterflies flitted once again. Jenky hadn't given her a real compliment since that fairy tale night of the hay ride. He didn't seem to realize that he had said anything special.

"Why do you call him *Reg*?" he asked. "It sounds like he's your best buddy."

"Because he asked me to call him that. If the man pays his rent, then I am happy. He's busy and so and am I." Jenky's hound dog look was pitiful. She should change the subject. "What else are you doing this summer besides trying to run things for me?"

Jenky looked around the crowd. "Vi, I owe it to your folks to keep you safe. Here you are this…lovely and healthy…young woman with no locks on your doors and a stranger living in your tack room. How can you be sure he's a big shot photographer?"

"Let's see…" She rubbed her chin. "I know; it's because he has a car full of equipment and he takes photos all day long."

"How much is the rent?"

"Why? Do you want to move in also?"

"How much?"

"Ten dollars, cash in advance."

"How long did he commit to stay and did you sign a contract?" He studied her face.

"Yes, in blood." Violet stuck her finger in a smear of icing and licked it off.

"I am serious, Vi."

"I know. That's your problem."

Jenky shuffled his feet. "This supper was delicious. I suppose you are cooking meals for *Reg*. Did I say that you look very fine in your dress-up clothes?"

Both of them reached for the box lid at the same time and their hands touched. They each withdrew instantly. Violet pretended to check the middle buttons down the front of her dress. The bodice had gotten tighter over the last few funerals.

Jenky leaned closer to her. "At the end of summer, you will have collected thirty dollars, provided he stays that long and you don't extend him credit. At that rate, you can buy your Sears home kit in about fifteen years. Then you'll need more money to have it assembled. Please, Vi, let me loan you the money."

"Fifteen years?"

"Yes, depending on the delivery charges."

"I'm not saving for the Sears house," she said quietly.

"What then?"

"Indoor plumbing."

Reggie walked past them and laid his hand on her shoulder. "Keeping it on the up and up here?"

Jenky frowned at him. "What's that supposed to mean?"

Reg grinned, big and broad. "Steady now. I'm only being friendly. Can't you take a joke?" He moved on, snapping a photo of Jenky as he left.

"See? He is a photographer."

Jenky looked her in the eye. "I want to install locks. It won't take me long at all. First thing tomorrow."

"I already gave you my answer. And what would that look like to Reg, anyway?"

Jenky's face twitched. She knew that twitch. He was working hard to keep his mouth shut. The Roberts family began tuning up their instruments for the dance and diners moved back their chairs.

"All will be well. I can handle everything, but thanks, Jenky. I appreciate your concern for my safety and the new work clothes. I really liked the note, too."

He stared at the table. "Could I have the first dance?"

"You mean if it's a slow one?"

"Right."

"As long as you've been coming to dances, have you ever heard them begin with a slow dance? You always ask for the first one."

"You never know." Jenky looked up. "Great. Here comes *Reg*."

Reg smiled at Violet. "You wanna dance?" The music, as she had predicted, was a lively jig, "Rory O'More". Tillie Roberts played the piano and her sons played banjo and accordion.

Violet glimpsed at Jenky. "Sure. Can you jig?"

Reg led her away. "With a name like Magee? You try and keep up."

Violet slipped off her shoes and Reg twirled her onto the floor. They were a blur of motion for the next four songs. She could keep up, but felt a pang of loss as Jenky left the room during the second song, not to return for slow dances or anything else that evening.

Jenky walked slowly past the Ford Roadster convertible with the New York license plates. He peeked inside. Nothing of interest. He kicked one of the tires, then put his hands in his pockets and went to his own pickup. Violet would be an easy target for a man of the world. It was his own fault that this was happening to her. He should have shared his true feelings with Vi many years ago rather than being about as romantic as a turtle, constantly withdrawing into his shell. He knew all about the law and the Colorado legislature, but she was right—Christmas cards don't count as letters and they for sure don't substitute for love letters. He had been a blockhead so now he would pay, and perhaps, dearly.

Jenky drove home at an unhurried pace, contemplating his situation.

Violet's place was coming up on the left. The moonlight revealed something odd on her mailbox. He slowed to a halt and was startled by a great-horned owl perched on top. It looked right at him, unblinking. Of all places for it to perch and at this particular moment, the owl had to be a sign from the Almighty. Jenky might be a cautious man, but even a cautious man must be wise enough to know when it was past time to take action. He should write her a letter and take his chances with her reaction. Could he actually write a once-in-a-lifetime love letter to her? Not likely, but there wasn't much to lose with Reg, the dashing dancer and romancer, in the wings. He put the truck in gear and floored it up and over the hill to his home. The owl flapped away as well.

~

The Butler house was one of the finest in the area. It was designed by Jenky's father in the latest style of Craftsman kit houses. The two-story house was made of wood and sandstone from a quarry in nearby Utah and brought to Dove Creek by wagon. When Irene and John moved from Pueblo, Colorado, to this new home in 1912, they brought Grandma Butler and baby Jenkins with them. Irene suffered from asthma and her husband's steel mill in Pueblo was a detriment to her health. He sold his interests and moved to Dolores County for the fresh air.

John didn't need the extra money, but he fenced his acreage and ran a big herd of cattle on the land. Irene called it his little amusement. Jenky was their only child and always had been a well-behaved and bright lad. John eventually sold the cattle, then had the land cleared and planted, most of it in pinto beans. The Stanley brothers, from on up the county road, had always put in the bean crop and harvested it for a fair share of the profits. John also had plumbing installed in the house. Now the place was locked up when Colorado's General Assembly was in session. During the summer, Jenky rattled around in it, reading, writing, and wishing Violet shared his name and his home.

Now he sat at his desk in the library composing the most difficult piece of legislation he'd ever attempted—an earnest accounting of his affection for Vi. His periodic pacing on the hardwood floor was accompanied by that of his brown and white Australian Shepherd, Caesar. Jenky gave him a good petting and then let him run outside for a bit. He wadded up the letter that he had been grinding out for the last few hours and started over. He paused only to ask for Divine help, several times.

⁓

Bean heard them coming. He went to the back door, ready to be let in, but it was a very long wait, even after the car stopped under a tree.

"I had fun tonight." Violet wondered what would happen next. "You are a swell dancer."

Reg rested his arm on the back of the seat. "I am a man of many talents. Dancing is but one."

"Really? Can you cook?"

He laughed. "You got me there but I'd like to get you over *here*," he said, patting the seat next to him. The moonlight beamed over his shoulder and she could see that a stray curl had fallen onto his forehead.

Bean meowed right next to Violet's side of the car and wouldn't stop.

Violet giggled. "I'm sorry. He's used to me being with him almost every minute."

"Lucky man." Reg took Violet's hand and kissed it. "Tomorrow then. I have the day off and I'd like to photograph you. I have a few prop clothes from my portrait-taking days. It'll be fun."

She was still shivering from the hand kissing. "I supposed that would be okay, but let's do that outdoors. I don't want anyone to get the wrong idea about us."

"Of course. That was my plan, too," he lied. "I'll come knocking about seven, then. We can have an early breakfast."

"Sure thing. Thank you for the wonderful evening, Reggie. Good night."

"I'll see you in my dreams."

She walked towards the back door with Bean prancing in the lead. Reg stayed in the car. Violet glanced back. She saw the glow of a match and smelled cigarette smoke soon after.

Chapter 3

Hog Herding

The noise didn't fit into Violet's dream about Bean and Jenky visiting the Dolores River Canyon overlook as someone screamed nearby. It was a man's voice. Violet sat up in her bed and listened. Yes, she definitely heard a man screaming and it was coming from the outhouse. She threw on her robe and work boots, grabbed her papa's shotgun off the rack and then clomped outside to see what was going on in the early morning light. Bean was at her side.

The screaming and yelling was mixed with grunting and snorting. Violet approached the privy with her gun cocked. "Come out of there, now, or I'm gonna shoot!" she yelled.

"Go ahead and shoot," Reg yelled back. "I'm being attacked anyway. I need help!"

"Inside the privy?" Violet yelled as she lowered her gun. As she did, a fat hog stuck his muddy snout around the corner of the outhouse and stared. Violet giggled and called the hog towards her with a loud *Soo-ey*. Bean disappeared under Reg's car. The hog trotted towards the car and snuffled around the tires.

"The coast is clear now; he's moved on to something else. You can come out," Violet shouted.

"I am not coming out until that monster is dead," Reg answered. "It chased me in here."

Violet laughed. "I will keep him away from you. It's only a hog."

"Hog to you. Monster to me."

"I'll get some feed and lure him away." She went to the house, put her gun away, and then grabbed the scrap bucket. But when she returned to the scene, the hog was gone.

She walked around the outhouse, the car, the barn, and the front yard, but he wasn't in sight.

"The pig is gone, Reg. Come on out. I'll walk you to the tack room."

"I'm not dressed. Are you sure it's gone?" His voice was scratchy from yelling.

"I don't see it or hear it. I'll go inside so you can leave. Holler if you need me." She couldn't help snickering to herself as she turned towards the house. As soon as she was inside, she watched out the window. After a few minutes, Reg came out wearing his skivvies. She quickly looked away.

❧

When he came for breakfast, Reg wasn't smiling. "I suppose you thought I was a big sissy about the pig."

"No, no." Violet was keeping a straight face. "He's a large one. I can see how a city man would be caught off guard."

"That's true. It could happen to anybody." He settled in for eggs and bacon. "Anyway, we should put that aside and concentrate on the day ahead."

Apparently he wasn't going to thank her for rescuing him. She smiled and ate her oatmeal.

He watched her. "Do you own any makeup?"

"I have some lipstick somewhere. Why?"

"Let's do some Hollywood shots for fun. You are glamorous enough to be a movie star. With makeup and a fancy dress you would put Hedy Lamarr to shame."

She blushed. "I don't have a fancy dress plus the lipstick is probably dried up by now."

He touched her nose with his finger and grinned. "Ah, but remember, I have a trunk full of both."

"What's the point in taking pictures of me anyway? You don't need Hollywood shots for *National Geographic*."

Reg set his coffee cup in the dishpan. "They…we…want to…capture the strong work ethic as well as the natural beauty of this area. You certainly qualify in both those departments."

Violet filled the dishpan with their plates and utensils. "If that's what you are looking for, then me putting on makeup would be the opposite of natural. And it's natural for me to wear overalls."

He stood very close to her. "Do you ever wear your hair down?" he asked, playing with her braid. "That would be more natural than a braid."

She moved her braid to the side. "I have been known to wear my hair down on occasion."

"Then do it today, please. Early start to catch the morning glow."

She kissed his cheek. "My chores are done, so I'll find that lipstick."

He drew a ragged breath and left.

❧

Violet brushed her hair in front of the mirror. She took the lid off the lipstick tube and rolled it up. It looked okay and didn't smell funny. She slowly drew the tube across her lips, then puckered up with a giggle. The dress Reg had picked out from his props was laying across her bed and the red shoes with the bow were a perfect fit. She was Cinderella.

⁓

Reg whistled when she came out to the front porch where he waited, smoking a cigarette. The light was good there, he had told her. He went straight to work, posing her, adjusting her chin and head, moving around her like a sheepdog again, arranging her hair, and giving her directions for the "look" he wanted with each shot.

"Lick your lips. Aces. Now let's head out into the countryside. The sun won't wait." He handed Violet a beautiful umbrella with lacy designs and a bamboo handle.

She opened it and followed him to the nearest field behind the barn. "I'm getting dust all over these fancy shoes."

"Don't worry about the shoes. Walk away from me and hold the umbrella a little higher. I want to see the top of your head. Pull your hair to the front so I can see your neck. That's it. Aces, Violet. Aces. That dress is really swell on you." He took loads of photos. "Look away towards the trees. Now look down, like a shy girl."

"You think it will rain if I hold this umbrella long enough?" she said, giggling. Something about this situation made her giddy. The dress was not new and had several snags in the fabric. It was a red and gold print with tiny buttons up the front and a black inset waist. It barely covered her knees. Someone must have whacked off the original length with scissors and didn't bother to do it properly with a new hem. Wearing fake clothes and hoisting an umbrella when the bean plants needed rain was foolish. At least he was taking the photographs in her back field. Nobody could see them.

"Let's head down to those trees now," Reg said as he reloaded his camera. "Can you carry the makeup bag?"

I suppose I can." Her hair bounced around her shoulders with each step. "I carry hay, cut posts, shovel manure, and run a bean farm."

He began snapping pictures. "Keep that attitude and look at me over your shoulder again. Ring-a-ding-ding, ginchy girl."

"What?"

"Ginchy girl. It means sexy."

"What? I can't hear you."

A crow near the creek below cawed repeatedly as Violet and Reg descended.

◁

"This is the best light." Reg moved around an outcropping of rocks by the creek. "I want you to sit on one level and lean against another. But first, let's add more makeup. There's a mirror and a cloth in the bag."

Violet spread a fabric square on the rock and carefully laid out the contents of the bag. She had used similar products her senior year in high school but not after Jenky left for college. What was the point? At this moment, she didn't know where to start.

"Why couldn't I have done this at the house?" she asked, dusting her face with powder.

"If we are outdoors, the light will affect how much you should wear. Not so much on your nose, kiddo." He smoothed the excess away with his fingers.

Violet gulped. His fingertips were velvety and warm. She couldn't remember a man ever touching her face, except when Jenky kissed her all those times in one night. But even then, only their lips touched.

Rather than apply the lipstick with the tube, Reg covered his own fingertip with the deep red color. "Part your lips a little," he said, his eyes all over her. "It will seem more natural if I do it this way." He gently outlined Violet's mouth. "You have full lips. Men like that."

"What men?" she said, only it came out *uuht eh* since her lips were transfixed. His breath was on her like steam from a hot kettle. She closed her eyes and he kissed her until she tasted tobacco. Even that didn't make her less enthusiastic, and when the kiss was over, she leaned in for another, even longer one.

Reg came to his senses first. "You are one red hot tomato," he said and turned greedy eyes on her again.

Violet was confused. "I am sorry. Is the lipstick smeared?"

He smiled. "Minor detail. I can put more on. But we will miss the light if I don't get busy. Let's finish this 'cup of tea' later, kiddo. Lean against that rock but pretend that you are lying in a bed of flowers on a warm summer day."

She snickered. "Sure. Farmers do that a lot."

He inhaled. "Do it for me, Sweet Lips. These poses are just for kicks anyway."

~

Jenky had seen King's hog earlier in the week. King of Prussia Lewis was the town junkyard owner, trash collector, dog catcher, car repairman, and big-time hog farmer. His parents had named him after their hometown in Pennsylvania. Before The Depression, King had at least one hundred pigs on his place. Now his biggest boar had escaped and wandered up Jenky's lane, making Caesar bark and wait anxiously by the door.

Jenky finally took pity on him. "You want to practice your herding skills, boy?" he said, scratching behind Caesar's ears. "Let's see what we can do to return this big fella back to his owner. You think you're all set for a trek up a couple of hills?"

Caesar's nails clicked on the hardwood floor as he scurried back and forth from the door to Jenky's desk. He watched as his master changed from his regular shoes to his farm boots and reached for the binoculars, draping the leather strap around his neck. They had belonged to Jenky's father.

"Easy, now, boy," Jenky said, grabbing his fedora. "This is not a sheep or a calf. This hog may give you trouble."

As soon as the door opened, Caesar was out. "Wait," Jenky said and Caesar hunkered down. King's hog paused also in his snooping around the vegetable garden gate. "Steady," Jenky said softly to Caesar. If they could get the hog to the back lane and out in the open, Caesar could herd him across the creek and up towards King's farm and then home. Jenky used voice commands because he never learned the whistles that his dad used with Caesar's mother. Caesar didn't need much help anyway. He had the fat pig trotting across a tractor turn row in about ten minutes. Jenky was right behind.

Crossing the creek could be a bother, but the spring runoff was about gone and there had been no rain. The animals could at least catch a drink there. The trio veered to the left and the gentle slope towards the creek. The hog appeared to enjoy the company and only stopped to snuffle around piñon and cedar tree trunks. Jenky was about to direct Caesar over a shallow area of the creek when he heard laughter not far away. "Hold," he said. Caesar rested not far from the hog.

Jenky walked a little ways from them and scrambled up a large rock. He raised his binoculars and scanned the creek. His view fell upon a man and woman kissing next to the creek. The woman was wearing a dress and her long, brown hair cascaded down her back. The man was blond and…Jenky adjusted the lenses as his jaw clinched. The woman was Violet. Her hair was down, she was wearing a bright dress, and she was the woman kissing that hotshot photographer.

The binoculars dropped out of Jenky's hands and swung like a pendulum across his chest. His mind swirled in shock. He plunked down hard on the rock. His love letter was useless now. Violet was lost to him.

It was then that he heard Caesar barking and the pig squealing. He leaped off the rock and headed back to where he left them. The clamor had moved to the creek. Jenky spotted Caesar just as the dog cornered the pig at a curve in the muddiest part of the shallow creek bed.

"Wait." Jenky shouted. Caesar looked back at him and then ran to his side, huffing and puffing. The pig flopped into the mud and wallowed as Caesar drank from the creek. But before Jenky could settle his own heart and mind, Caesar took off after the pig again. The hog gained his footing and careened farther down the creek, squealing.

Jenky ran along his side of the creek and yelled out Caesar's name. He rounded another turn in time to see the hotshot Reg lose his cap while running and screaming like a wild man a few yards ahead of the pig. Violet was still at the kissing scene, laughing. When Jenky arrived, her jaw dropped and she began gathering up Reg's equipment in shocked silence. Jenky had never seen anyone so beautiful. He could not move until Caesar returned and licked his hand. Jenky turned away from Violet's presence and began the long walk home.

He had seen them. Violet saw the dazed, wounded expression on Jenky's face. Her initial reaction was to go to him with consoling words, but then she remembered her decade of lonesome nights with the Sears catalog, waiting for him to offer a sign that he cared. She didn't have it in her to wait any longer. So, rather than offer consolation, she made her way up her side of the creek until she couldn't feel his pain quite so intensely. She looked back and saw him walking with his head down like an old mule. Jenky had his chance. Now it was Reg's.

Chapter 4

Social Skills

*V*iolet found Reg sitting in his car, fuming. She could lighten him up. She smiled, but not in a mocking way. "Is there a pig in your past you'd like to talk about?" She handed his cap through the window.

"No." He took the cap and then lit up a cigarette. "Either that beast goes or I'm finding someplace else to stay."

How could he say that after they'd kissed? She couldn't let that happen. Not now. "I'll take care of it. There are leftovers in the cupboard. I may be gone awhile, okay?"

"Yeah. Did I see you with a gun the other day?"

Violet nodded. So, he had seen her in her robe then. "Why?"

"I'd like to have it here with me while you are gone in case that thing comes back."

He was serious. "You would shoot it? That *beast* belongs to someone who makes his living raising hogs. You can't decide to shoot someone's property."

"I can if it is attacking me and off the owner's property. Pigs can be mean." Reg jumped as two hens got into a spat near his car. "This place is a distraction to my work."

Violet shooed the hens away. "Have you ever shot a gun?"

He blew a big puff of smoke. "Just forget it. I'll wait here until you get back."

"You want me to walk you to your room or inside the house?" Normally, she would have found this conversation humorous, but she didn't want to lose him. "I don't mind if you wait inside."

He tossed his cigarette out the window. "All right. Lead the way, then. I can eat something while I wait."

～

Violet searched around for the elusive pig but didn't want to waste too much time on the effort. She drove into Dove Creek, hoping that King might be in town. His truck wasn't around. That meant a trip to his house was necessary. As the crow flies, his pig farm wasn't that far from her farm, but his actual entrance was off a different county road. King lived on the hill above her and in the opposite direction of Jenky, but thankfully, King's place was out of sight. She hadn't been there for years and she didn't want to go now. It smelled disgusting, horrible. He collected trash and mean, stray dogs. Most folks considered King to not be right in the head. He lived as close as you could get to the cemetery without actually living in your grave. People tried to choose a day to bury their loved ones when the wind was blowing towards King's farm. They rarely succeeded.

King's half-house, half-shack was colorful since he had covered the sides and roof with discarded license plates. His huge 4 X 4 truck was heaped to the top of its wooden sideboards with tin cans, bottles, and other garbage. Somewhere under that trash was a snow plow that he attached to the big truck in the winter to clear out roads for neighbors. Violet drove the Maxwell close to the front door. Half a dozen dogs were going crazy, jumping on her car and barking. Surely King would come out to see what the ruckus was about. Big flies buzzed around her window.

"Hey, shut up!" he yelled at the dogs from the screen door. They sauntered off. King was fastening his overall straps over his union suit and smoking a cigar. His mostly white hair resembled the roots of a green onion. "Who is it?" He shaded his eyes towards Violet's car. "You're the Hendricks girl. Where are your overalls? You gettin' married or buried today?" He pushed open the screen and stepped outside. She had forgotten how exceptionally tall he was. He leaned in the passenger window. There was food caught in his moustache and beard. He reeked of liquor and pig muck.

"Well, what is it?" he asked. "I'm fresh out of tea and lemonade, but I got some whiskey." He laughed, coughed, and spat.

"Look, King, if you're missing a big boar hog, I know where he is," Violet said quickly, then went right back to holding her breath.

He took the cigar out of his mouth. "You're a right handsome woman in a dress and lip coloring. So, where's my pig?"

"At my farm and he's becoming a nuisance to my boarder."

"Is that a fact? You want me to do something about this situation, I suppose. I'll take him off your hands when you marry Jenky Butler."

Violet put the car in reverse. The conversation had gone beyond her duty to Reg.

"I'm kidding." King guffawed. "Scared ya, didn't I? You ever gonna get hitched to the Butler boy?" He blew cigar smoke into the car. "You wouldn't have far to go if the wedding was at his big house."

She winced at the smoke. "When I marry, it will be someone of my choice. Can you fetch your hog today?"

"That boy is backward—socially, I mean."

Violet's eyes widened at King's bold assessment. As though he would know.

"He's too smart to be sociable. Is that your problem with him? As for me, I can tolerate anybody if I'm not around them a lot." His big belly jiggled with laughter at his own wittiness. "I'll be over to get my boar. He's probably skinny by now after being gone a solid week. You've taken a shine to your boarder, and that's why you're all gussied up." King saluted her, spat, and went inside his colorful house.

Violet stepped on the gas and shot backwards, narrowly missing King's license-plated outhouse. His pack of dogs ran out from under his porch as if to defend the privy. She shifted gears and jostled down the road.

~

Reg had better appreciate what she'd endured to keep him safe from a silly hog. Why hadn't she taken the time to change clothes before leaving home? Now King would tell anybody who would listen that she was gussying up because she was sweet on her renter. Gosh. She didn't have a chance to change because Reg was suffering an unmanly tizzy. What made King think that she was sweet on him? The box social. She knew it was King's habit to lurk in a corner at the Grange Hall, watching the fun. She shouldn't have jigged every fast dance with Reggie Magee.

Now she must deal with the image of Jenky watching the fun she and Reg had by the creek. She would never get his rejected, dejected face nor his old mule walk, out of her mind. But even King knew that Jenky had the social skills of a pinto bean unless he was running for office.

Only one other car met her on the road home. She got out at her mailbox. Nothing there. She surveyed the horizon, but not a rain cloud in sight. As she made her way down the lane, Violet spotted the culprit pig taking a nap under the Farmall. Good. He probably was so tired from chasing Reg that he would sleep until his owner came to fetch him. Bean was also asleep on his rug in the kitchen. There were dirty dishes on the table and ashes in a saucer.

~

She found Reg resting on the loveseat, reading her comic book. He grinned and put out his cigarette. "This Superman character is rip-snorting. Do you have the next issue?"

"No. I get used issues from Denver. Did you get that out of my bedroom?"

He came towards her with his arms out. "Let's finish what we started earlier—a little bill and coo. I've had a bad scare."

She forgot about the comic book and let him kiss her. He could sure use some of her tooth powder after all those cigarettes. But more than that, he shouldn't have been in her bedroom. His kisses were exciting, but not thrilling to her core. Not like on a certain hayride.

Right in the middle of their third kiss, Reg picked her up and carried Violet to her bedroom. She wiggled out of his arms and fell on the bed. "What are you doing?" She quickly rolled over and sat up. You aren't supposed to be in here."

He jumped on top of her and wrestled her into a passionate kiss.

"Get off me—now!" She shoved him hard.

He stumbled off and stood over her. "What's your story, morning glory? Afraid to fool around a little? Are you in love with Mr. Deep Pockets?"

Her face prickled from his overnight stubble or something. She went straight to the kitchen and began cleaning up his dishes.

Reg followed and decided to humor her. "Actually, I should get this film off to the developer. Is the pig owner coming soon?"

"You talking about me?" King said with his face plastered against the screen.

Reg jumped. "Have you not heard of knocking, you lame-brain? What do you want?"

"I want my pig back. Where's Violet? Hope you haven't moved into the house. Wait," he whispered and put his hand up to his ear. "That rumbling sound must be her folks rolling in their graves."

Violet came to the door, her cheeks rosy. "Hello again. I didn't think you would get here so fast."

King grinned. "So I see. I had me a woman once, but the hogs ran her off. Nobody ever saw her again." He made a scary face and mimicked ghostly sounds as he wiggled his fingers towards Reg.

Violet pushed on the screen door and went outside, pointing to the Farmall. "Your hog is under my tractor, at least he was ten minutes ago."

"I'll get him." He smiled knowingly at Violet and smashed a fly on his arm. "That fella in there is full of malarkey and a high hat, too. I can spot 'em and I'm never wrong about people or pigs. Jenky is a thousand times the man."

She blushed.

"Don't be doing him any favors, missy. I'm a malarkey man myself, but only in jest. He's out to chisel somebody."

"Please just get your hog and go home, King. I don't have anything worth chiseling."

He angled his head and looked at her with one eye shut. "I wouldn't be too sure about that, young lady."

Violet watched him call softly to the pig. It raised its head and flicked an ear then trotted after King to his truck. He lifted out the wooden tailgate and then leaned it against the truck like a ramp. The pig sniffed around before walking right up it and into the truck bed. King gave him a pat on the head and inserted the ramp back into its place as a tailgate. Then he turned towards Violet, saluted, and made the scary face and ghost sounds again. He drove off laughing.

She headed back to the house as Reg came out. He had returned to his confident self.

"How about some food, woman? I'm starving," he said, and lifted Violet off her feet, swinging her around in circles.

She giggled so much that she didn't notice Tyrel Fetters was honking as he turned into her lane. "Put me down," she told Reg.

Tyrel beamed. He winked at Violet as she approached his truck.

"It sure is a fine day," he said, darting his beady eyes towards Reg.

"I assume you have mail for me." Violet's voice was wearing thin.

"Actually, I have a registered letter for your friend."

"What friend?"

Reg came up to her side. "I think he means me, kiddo." He took the letter and pencil from Tyrel and scribbled his name on the line. "Thanks, pal." Reg took the letter and strode across to the tack room.

"See you, Tyrel," Violet said, hoping for a quick retreat.

"Never seen you dressed up like this. Even got eye makeup on." He shrieked out a wolf whistle. "Sorry to interrupt your little frolic," Tyrel said, running his tongue over his teeth. "Boy, howdy, you sure move fast once you decide to move."

"I was modeling for him. He is a photographer for National Geographic and it's none of your business." She took the first few steps a little too fast and tripped in the high heels. She grabbed at her short skirt.

Tyrel jumped out to help. "Easy does it." He tittered. "Modeling, huh? Wait until this news gets around. Does Jenky know?"

Violet shouldn't have answered at all. "I don't really care whether Jenky knows or not." She dusted her hands as Jenky's forlorn face popped up in her mind. "Any news?"

"Not much today. They picked a Typical American Family at the New York World's Fair. The winner is a Leathers family from Texas and they are farmers. That's about it. Take it slow now, Violet." Tyrel laughed, made a U-turn, and left.

She went inside and changed into her overalls and braided her hair. While Reg was gone to the post office, she and Bean went to the pump at the windmill and got a bucket of water. Back inside, she dipped a square of flannel into the water and tried to wipe off the mascara and lipstick. Some of the lipstick wouldn't come off. So be it. Let Tyrel tattle to Jenky. The damage had been done. Her feet hurt from wearing the high heels.

At supper, Reg talked about his work in Hollywood before his current job at the *National Geographic Society*. "You would be shocked at how much makeup the stars wear. You wouldn't recognize some of them without it. You, however, are a true natural beauty. Great eyebrows and lashes, high cheekbones, and brilliant red highlights in your hair. Directors would love you because you are perfect from every angle. Why haven't you been grabbed by some man before now?"

Violet had never had so many compliments at once, but she resented the man comment. "I've been busy making this farm work. It is a hard way to make a living but I did it, and time just got away from me. I'm not much of a party girl. I love it out here and I wouldn't want to be anywhere else. But if we don't get some rain soon, we will all lose our crops. I don't know what will happen then." She paused. "I do know that communities stick together out here and help each other. Everybody shared everything during this gosh-awful depression. Are you finished with your food?"

⌒

Reg lit up, even though he could tell she didn't care much for smoking. He watched her move around the kitchen. What a beauty she was, but also a tough woman to run this farm alone. There had to be many forlorn nights, especially in the winter when the snow was deep. He had messed up by putting moves on her in the bedroom. That wasn't the way to her heart. She might need heavy doses of romance before anything more could be possible. He would have to break out his book of poetry and start getting her to dance along to the car radio.

~

"Have you ever entered a beauty contest?" Reg asked one morning at breakfast.

Violet laughed. "Someone nominated me for the Prettiest Eyes Contest in high school, but I didn't win." She finished up her oatmeal.

"Bunch of nitwits. Who could have eyes prettier than yours?"

"Lots of people, especially Alma Funk. Hers were as light blue as the sky, like she was an angel."

He took her hand, swallowing the last of his eggs and toast. "You are the only angel I've ever known."

"You always have the right words at the right time, Reg." Violet shuddered as he kissed her palm.

"The right words come easy around you, babe. Tonight we will listen to music on my car radio and watch the stars. If the right song comes on, we can get out and slow dance."

"That sounds romantic. Where are you working today?" Violet asked.

"Over the border in Utah. How about you?"

She stacked the dishes into the dishpan and stoked up the wood stove. "I am chopping weeds," she said as she filled a kettle with the water bucket. "I saw plenty of Russian thistle and bindweed in the fields the other day. It grows whether it rains or not."

"Watch out for giant hogs." He put on his cap and kissed her goodbye.

~

Violet leaned against the table, waiting for the water to get hot. This must be what it's like to be married, well, almost. Then why didn't she miss him more when he was out doing his job? Why didn't she dream about him at night? She set the dishpan on the sideboard and drizzled homemade soap over it from a jar. The pot of water began steaming. She lifted it with two dishtowels and poured it over the pan of plates, cups, and utensils. "Wonder what Jenkins Butler is doing right now?" she asked Bean.

When she was done drying the dishes, Violet brought in the washtub from the barn and then carried in several more buckets of water and more wood inside so things would be ready for her bath after a day in the fields later. She set the dishpan on the still-hot stove and filled it with water. It might still be a little warm when she came home. She made herself a bread and butter sandwich, filled her canteen, put all that and a couple of leftover sugar cookies and some grapes in her lunch pail.

She turned the cow out to pasture before sharpening her hoe and putting on her gloves and straw hat. She was getting a very late start.

                          ~

Glenn and Jim Stanley had run the Butler farm since Jenky went off to college. The Stanley men were jovial, big, and honest to the core. Jenky loved them like family. This particular morning, Jenky and the brothers were discussing the prospect of a drought. They had been talking for an hour about the situation.

"Sounds like you aren't gonna stick around for the summer," Glenn said. "Won't that be a first since you were in college?"

Jim raised an eyebrow. "That fact got anything to do with Violet's renter?"

Jenky poured them all more coffee and returned to his chair at the table before responding.

"I have details for one of my proposed bills to iron out in Denver. I need access to documents and law books. That kind of thing."

Glenn shook his head. "Come on, Jenky. You've been carrying a torch for Vi since we were kids." He hesitated. "Man, that's been a lot of years. Isn't it time for you to do something about it before this slick stranger runs off with her?"

"Plenty of fellas around here have tried to court her over the years, but she won't have it." Jim added. "Clara says Violet's had a candle burning for you, too, but everybody has limits as to how long they can wait. You're gonna regret it if all you do is run away, cause we all know that's what you are about to do."

Jenky shrugged. "Guilty, your honor. Count me with the chickens, I suppose. Between us guys, I was gonna propose to her this summer, but then this photographer twit showed up. It's obvious that she's really taken with him." He didn't reveal why he was so sure about that.

"Well, it's your business." Glenn looked at his watch. "We'd better get going. I'm just saying Violet is a God-fearing woman and she showed everybody that she can run a farm. But as good looking as she is, if the renter doesn't steal her, somebody else is bound to. Bessie says that Violet is too smart to hang around forever. I don't get it, man."

"Your wife's got a valid point. If Violet needs anything at all this summer, you two take care of it. Go by and just say hello if you have to. I don't trust this stranger at all with her. Bessie and Clara could pay a call with some excuse that Vi could swallow."

"Want us to take care of *all* your concerns, eh?" Jim said and put on his hat. "You gotta hand it to Violet, she's been alone all this time for what...a bean farm and a friendly nod from you now and then."

Glenn took one more sip of coffee and stretched. "Must be hard for a lawyer to take advice, but we're kinder than most folks in the county would've been. Lots of talk going around about the photographer and Vi. Thought you should know."

Jenky looked him in the eye. "If I am out of the picture, the gossip might let up somewhat. You'd be the first to be aware if anything untoward is going on that would hurt her. Let me know. I am not cut out for romance, I guess. Could be that it's for the best for me to take a hike."

"You sure are dumb for a smart guy," Jim said. "Ever consider she might be trying to make you jealous to force you into something?"

He had already thought of that. "You two get out of here." They all pushed back their chairs and moved towards the door. "I hope and pray it rains so you can get your money out of this year's crop," Jenky said and they shook hands. "Thanks for the advice. I do appreciate your thoughts about Violet and me."

~

Jenky watched the Stanleys drive away while he rubbed Caesar's ears. "How about we go for a walk? No hogs to herd this time."

He put on his hat, work boots, and his faithful binoculars. Caesar had already run back and forth from the door to his master five times before they made it outside at last.

Caesar marked every bush and tree he could, and Jenky used his binoculars to see what, if any, progress the beans were making. Not much. He did spot a rabbit and watched as a red-tail hawk flew overhead and landed on a fencepost separating his and Violet's fields. That rabbit had better keep his wits about him. Caesar saw the hawk, too, and moved slowly in his direction then ran at his perch, causing the hawk to take flight and the rabbit to seek cover in the nearby vegetation along Dove Creek. Jenky called Caesar back and gave him a pet.

"Ready for a drink, boy?" Jenky asked. "Let's detour to the creek, then." They walked along the same trail as the day he'd seen Violet kissing her fellow. He tried to blot out that scene, but it was impossible. He noticed Caesar was ahead of him when he heard him barking in a friendly way. Sure enough, through his binoculars he saw Violet sitting on a fallen log hugging Caesar. Her lunch pail was open next to her. Jenky whistled for his dog. He couldn't bring himself to go down to look her in the eye after that kiss. Things between them would never be the same.

∾

Jenky had kept the love letter under lock and key in his bureau drawer. He should probably burn it now but he didn't. Somehow he felt as long as those words, so very long in coming, were on paper, there was still hope that God and Vi would have mercy on him. Goodness knows that the way things stood, it would take a miracle for Violet to love him after Reg had motivated her to wear her hair unbraided. Now all could be lost and it was because he couldn't say certain words to her in person.

∾

Violet knew that if Caesar was running around, Jenky wasn't far behind. Her throat tightened and she waited for him to appear but he never did. Instead, she heard the whistle that perked up Caesar's ears and caused him to cast a quick look at her, then dash back up the path to his master. Tears dropped onto Violet's overalls. Could he not at least talk to her about Reg? They had yelled at one another for almost twenty-eight years. Why stop now? She knew it was because she had let her hair down and it wasn't for him. Jenky was a special, private man. Some other girl would be lucky when she found that out.

Some other girl would be wiser and see that Jenky couldn't take risks when it came to love. He couldn't speak with his heart like he did with his mind on the floor of Colorado's General Assembly in Denver. It would take a special woman to see that she would have to do the talking and ask him to marry her so that all lonely evenings on the front porch, in the parlor, and anywhere else would be over. That other, wiser girl's lonely evenings would be spent laughing and talking about the future, about literature and music, about hope, and about love. *Oh, Jenky*. She covered her face and bawled.

Chapter 5

Rainy Days

*S*unrise found Violet gathering eggs. She saw his pickup creep past. She waved but he was looking straight ahead or so it seemed. Where would he be going this early in the morning? Even Sitton's wouldn't open for another hour. Reg had come in late, after she had gone to bed. His rent was due and she was thinking of a clever way to remind him.

She heard the tack room door open and peeked between the slats of the henhouse. Reg came stumbling out, still in his clothes, and behaving very drunk. His curly hair stuck out like a dandelion gone to seed. Violet squeezed her eyes shut as Reg decided to forego a trip to the privy and, to her dismay, relieved himself on her wheelbarrow that was leaned against the corral. How rude. Forget about a clever way of reminding him that his rent was due. She would come right out and ask for it. He could fix his own breakfast, too. She had more weeds to chop in the field.

~

It was around noon when she heard the first rumble. At first, it didn't register in her mind that it was thunder. It was from a bank of shadowy clouds stretching fully across the western horizon. Violet whooped and jumped for joy, then gathered up her hoe and her lunch pail. A sudden gust of wind swept her hat off and it turned like a pinwheel over empty rows of beans and came to rest upside down, like a vessel ready to catch the rain. She ran as fast as she could to the house. There were things to do before a storm.

~

Violet took care of everything before it hit. She and Bean were watching out the kitchen door as the first lightning strike came close—probably on the sloping hillside of Jenky's place. The thunder was tremendous. Reg shot out of the tack room and set about putting the top up on his car. She decided to help him. Once it was on, he rolled up the windows and they ran inside the house. There was no gradual beginning of the rain; it began pouring right from the start.

They sat at the table, eyes glued to the window. Reg smoked a cigarette and Violet ran to close the window in her bedroom. Bean went with her and curled up on the bed. When Violet turned around, Reg was leaning on the door jamb with his arm stretched across the opening.

"What time is it?" he asked.

Violet passed under his arm. "The clock is there, on the desk."

"Are you mad at me?"

"Why would I be?"

"Sorry I came home late. I was talking with some men who live just outside Monticello and we were…"

"Drinking? Monticello is a Mormon town."

Reg laughed. "I'm fairly sure those cowboys weren't Mormons. One of them had a dog named Turk. He said its real name was Turkey Butkus, but his wife made him call it Turk. She might have been a Mormon. What's wrong, Violet?" He pulled her to him.

He smelled of liquor. "Your rent was due yesterday."

Reg held her back by her shoulders. "You are mad about that? I can get it for you right now. Don't move." He ran outside in the downpour. He returned, drenched, but holding out a wet ten dollar bill in the kitchen. "Here. All's well now."

She took the damp money to her room and returned with a blanket for him. "You are shivering."

"Want to warm me up?"

She ignored him. "It's so dark and cold. I'll get the stove going. Could you bring in more wood from that big bin on the front porch?"

He opened the front door and she heard the rain drumming heavily on the porch floor. Reg closed the door with his foot and stacked the wood next to the stove. He covered himself with the blanket while Violet got the fire going. They pulled their chairs close to the stove.

She decided to get it out in the open. "I don't approve of drinking, and I think you came home drunk. But what you do away from here is your business, I was just upset. I knew that you would pay your rent."

"I see." He sneezed. "At least you are honest."

She smiled. "Now tell me about your trip."

~

The rain continued into the evening. Violet lit lamps throughout the house. They played dominoes and drank coffee in the dim glow. He went to the tack room again, wearing her winter coat over his head and brought back his book of poems. He read some aloud to her until she yawned behind her hand.

He stopped. "Do you have to milk that cow tonight?"

"No," she yawned again. "I milk her once a day. I cleaned her stall and gave her hay. Same thing with the chickens. I'm not sure if Bean will like going outside in the rain for his bathroom break though."

Reg laughed. "I know how he feels."

"There's a bucket under your bed. Haven't you noticed it?"

"Nope, but I'll find it."

She opened the cupboard door. "We can have beans and biscuits. I planned to go to the ice house today, but that didn't work out."

"Canned beans in bean country? That's a laugh."

"Home-canned beans, silly. I wouldn't feed you store-bought beans." She busied herself with making biscuit dough.

Reg lined up dominoes on the table and tipped the first one over for the chain reaction. "Either your cat doesn't like this clatter or he needs to go really bad."

"This is a downpour," she said, shooing Bean onto the screened-in porch for a minute. Outside, the raindrops peppered the ground so hard that each splashed back up like the Old Faithful geyser she'd seen in a movie reel. Bean meowed in protest. "Poor kitty. Just be glad you have a box of dirt out here rather than out there. I've never seen a rain like this."

Reg made another line of dominoes. "I plan to shoot some pictures of Monument Valley and visit trading posts on the Navajo Reservation— hopefully documenting the family life over there. My boss likes the idea. I may have to sleep in my car for a week. You should give me some food to take since I already paid my rent in advance."

She set their plates and forks on the table. "You'll be gone a week? When?"

He shrugged. "I'm thinking next week. That okay with you?"

"Of course. I went there once in high school with…a friend's family. It's really something. Don't get lost." Bean meowed and Violet let him in. She rubbed him dry with a clean rag, then stood up.

Reg put his arms around Violet's waist and kissed her. "Will you miss me?"

She tossed the damp rag towards the door. "Of course."

He kissed her ear. "Would it be all right if we sit on that uncomfortable granny chair in there?"

She giggled. "It's called a loveseat."

"Then we should put it to good use." Reg led her into the parlor and they cuddled up on the hard cushion. "Are you cold? I could get that blanket."

"No. I'm fine. Let's listen to the rain until the biscuits are done."

"Sure. Whatever you want," Reg mumbled as he kissed her neck.

Violet wasn't sure what she wanted. Her gaze fell on the Sears Newcastle floor plan and the ad that showed the Jenky-type man shaving in his fancy bathroom. Which did she want more, the indoor plumbing or the man?

Reg was getting too friendly on the loveseat.

She wriggled out of his grasp. "I'd better check on the biscuits. The stove was a little too hot."

~

The storm didn't let up. Reg had to get soaked again when he went to the tack room for the night. Violet put another quilt on her bed and lay awake wondering what Jenky would have been doing on the road at sunrise. He did that at the end of every summer when he returned to Denver but never in the middle of…she sat straight up…Jenky was going back early because of Reg.

Bean jumped on the bed with her, purring above the noise of the rain. She stroked his velvety head. It wasn't Reg's fault. She was the one who had let her hair down.

~

The rain continued through the next day and didn't move along until mid-morning of the third day. Violet had cleaned the barn stall, pulled down fresh hay from the loft and was cleaning out the henhouse when Tyrel honked outside the tack room. Reg came out and signed for another envelope. Tyrel was halfway through his U-turn when he stopped.

"Hello, Peaches," he said with the *s* whistling between his protruding teeth. "The creek's overflowed from here to the river, the state road into Cortez is underwater, there's a mudslide on the ice house road, and Jenky has gone back to Denver. That's the news. Which one of those tidbits is most upsetting?"

Violet lifted a bale of hay off the wheelbarrow and snipped the wires. "I needed ice two days ago."

"Looks like it will be two more, missy." He pointed up the hillside behind her. "It appears part of King's farm is now on your land. Good luck with that." He finished his U-turn and, after fish-tailing a couple of times, headed on his way.

Violet lifted her rubber boots out of the muck and turned to see what

Tyrel was talking about. A mudslide had shaved the dirt from under several fence posts separating King's place from hers at the top of the hill. There wasn't a thing she could do about it.

~

Violet had to start the Farmall to make sure it hadn't gotten rain down the exhaust pipe. If it did, she would be in trouble. That's the one thing she had forgotten to do was run the tractor inside the barn before the storm. The tin can was still in place over the pipe, though. It started right away and the can flew straight up and over the side. She jumped down to retrieve it. Reg was standing there holding it like a prize.

"What's for supper?" he asked. "I'm thinking about potatoes. Do you have any?"

Violet took the can and stepped up on one of the front tires to replace it over the exhaust.

"I have potatoes but we also have leftovers to finish. Remember the soup? I'm keeping it warm on the stove. Help yourself , if you're hungry. There are biscuits in the cupboard."

"I was hoping for fried potatoes and onions"

"How about tomorrow? Can you help me reload the wood bin on the porch?"

"Me?" His brow knitted into a maze.

She giggled. "All you have to do is push the wheelbarrow around there. I loaded it already."

He lifted the handles and pushed it through the mud and around the side of the house. He smiled over his shoulder. "Farm life is a piece of cake," he said as the wheel hit a stone uncovered by the rain, flinging the wood and Reg onto the muddy, soggy ground.

Violet laughed hard as she went to rescue him. They laid the wood on the porch to dry before putting it in the bin. "Don't worry; it's not all that wet. You can still have your potatoes and onions tomorrow."

Reg seemed a bit sheepish. "We really want to get more photos of you tomorrow. I have another dress for you to wear."

Violet wiped her boots on the edge of the porch. "Why do you need to take my picture again?"

"The others didn't turn out right. Something went wrong during the processing. It won't take long. I know what we need."

"Who's this *we*?" Violet asked, removing her boots and gloves at the door. "You keep saying it."

"Do I, really?" He blushed. "It's a habit, the same as saying *aces*. I'm like a nurse who says, "How are *we* today?""

Violet checked the horizon. "No clouds in sight. Now *we* need sunshine to make those beans sprout. Take off your shoes before you come in." She went inside and he followed. "I'll get the stove fired up so you can eat the soup, but then I have to change out of these wet, muddy overalls and into my dry ones."

"A backup pair? What a surprise," he said with a big grin.

Violet turned her head slowly and stared him down. "I'm washing clothes tomorrow. You can use the water for yours when I'm done."

"What about a bath? I'm overdue."

"Sure." She smiled. "Just hop right in the tub before I pour the water out. I'll be hanging the clothes out on the line." She retrieved her washboard from a nail on the back porch and laid it on the table, as a reminder.

~

Violet stopped at Sitton's before getting ice in Cahone. Mrs. Sitton saw her come in. She was measuring fabric for a customer, but quickly turned that job over to her helper, Pauline. Violet squatted down to check something on a low shelf. That's where the bargains usually were.

"You can't hide from me." Mrs. Sitton stood over Violet with her hands on her hips. "Is it true that Jenky went back early because that boarder of yours got too friendly? He's not making you uncomfortable, is he? There are plenty of men around here who would sure pay a visit to your place and run him out of the county. You say the word." Her chin quivered with this proclamation.

Violet laughed as she stood. She gave her friend a hug. "I am fine. Who knows why Jenky went back to Denver. It's possible he has a girl there." She didn't meet Ethel's eyes.

"Jenky doesn't have any girl but you. He needs a mule to kick some sense into him so he will act on it. I'm worried about this boarder." She lowered her voice to a whisper. "You know how word gets around, Violet. He could cast doubt on your fine reputation."

Time to go. "I can handle my renter and you can handle the gossip for me. Here's my shopping list, if Pauline could fill it. I'll drop by after I pick up ice. Thank you." She gave Ethel a peck on her cheek.

〜

"I am not wearing this," Violet said and presented Reg with the powder blue dress he had asked her to wear for her latest picture-taking session.

Reg held up the floral dress with its heart-shaped buttons and lace-trimmed puff sleeves. "It looks great to me. Come on, what's the problem?"

He was, of course, quite aware of the problem so she gave him the scolding teacher look she had learned from her mother. "It is way too low cut and you know it. They should have added two more buttons at the top."

"You have to wear it, kiddo. We want this color. It will be very flattering in the afternoon light." He tossed the dress to her. "We don't have all day either."

"There you go with the 'we' again. Are these color pictures? I thought they would be black and white." She puckered her mouth to the side as she eyed the neckline.

"This is a special photo. It could be a full page in the National Geo," he said, then winked. "Give it another try."

Violet disappeared into the house. She returned wearing the dress and her work boots.

Reg snickered as he set up his tripod. "Very clever combo."

"This is supposed to be about farmers." She shrugged. "I'm a farmer."

"You're also a beautiful woman." He looked her up and down before kissing her soundly. "Wait a minute. What happened to the plunging neckline?" He frowned at the lacy substitution.

"Stop staring at me. I tucked in one of Mother's Sunday hankies. It's either that or back to a sturdy shirt and overalls."

He swore to himself. "Have it your way, then. I'm doing only close ups this time around. Stand over there by the porch post." He peered through his camera lens. "Did you pick up extra food for me to eat while I'm gone next week?"

"Yes, sir. I hope you are happy with my choices, since it's take-what-you're-given around here. They didn't have the shoestring potatoes in a can, for instance."

He wasn't listening. "Look at the camera like you know a big secret." The shutter clicked several times.

"What does knowing a big secret have to do with this kind of assignment?" Bean rubbed against Violet's work boots. She picked him up. She held the cat next to her cheek and smiled. "How about me with my best buddy?" The honeysuckle vine behind her smelled like Heaven.

"That's me, right?" He took one shot. "We are best buddies."

"I'm not sure what we are. I was hoping for something more romantic than buddies."

He flashed his charming smile. "I think that can be arranged since both parties are now interested."

"Really. Just like that? I haven't run you off with my hermit habits and overalls?" Her heart beat a little quicker.

"Nah. I know the real Violet Hendricks. She's a wild woman. Tilt your head back and laugh."

"About what? About me being a wild woman? I take that as an insult to my reputation."

He peeked around his camera. "Just *kidding*, jitterbug, as in me trying to make you laugh for the picture."

She thought about it, then tilted her head back and giggled. He snapped the pose several times.

"Aces. Really, Vi, that was perfection. So, what made you laugh?"

"I pictured King's hog chasing you up the hill." Did he just call her *Vi?* Nobody but Jenky called her *Vi* to her face. It didn't seem right for Reg to horn in on something that was special between the two of them.

Reg got quiet. "That's enough pictures for now." He placed his camera in its case and took down his tripod. "You shouldn't mock the fears of others. I was nearly killed by hogs one time."

Violet felt bad. It was dumb and uncalled for to bring up hogs. She touched his arm. "I'm sorry, Reg. Please forgive me."

He nodded and continued packing his equipment.

"It could make you feel better to tell me the story," she said, meaning it.

He leaned against the house, his head hanging low. "I was about seven years old and towards the end of summer, my two older brothers took me with them to a county fair. I thought we were all having fun, but evidently, I was being a pest and keeping them from flirting with the girls.

In the livestock tent, some men were setting up to have a greased pig race and my brothers decided to enter me in it. But first they each bought a double-dip of vanilla ice cream and stuck it all right smack into my hair. The two of them made sure every hair was saturated and dripping with ice cream as the piggies were released.

So, when the race began, I was already crying and tripping over the other kids who were chasing the half-dozen piglets. Once I was on the ground and those slick little porkers discovered the ice cream in my hair, it was a nightmare of pig snouts and licking that I'll never forget." He trembled. "The sounds still haunt me."

Violet truly thought that Reg was going to cry. She was trying so hard not to laugh that the only decent thing she could do was put her arms around him and start kissing. So she did.

~

No sooner had Jenky arrived at his apartment near the Capitol Building than he wished he were home. How would he know the goings on in Dove Creek if he was in Denver? What foolishness to allow himself to be ruled by negative emotions. That wasn't his normal course of action. Now he was stuck. The first thing he did was to call Ethel Sitton and make her his confidante. She was to give him a weekly report as well as call whenever it was necessary. Ethel didn't spread gossip as such, but she certainly got an earful of it at her store. Jenky and Caesar took a rest after the day's ride over the mountains, and then they went out for a walk. One of his colleagues and his dog were just returning from a stroll.

Jenky enjoyed matching wits with other legislators who lived in the mansion. They talked politics and issues over meals and enjoyed an occasional poker game. He often thought that he would bring Violet to Denver, perhaps take in a play at Elitch Gardens, dance slow dances at the Trocadero Ballroom, and dine at the Brown Palace. He never got that particular bill out of his committee of one and onto the floor to see what Vi might think of such a plan.

Of course if he could ever bring himself to propose marriage, his Denver scenario would be a perfect honeymoon. They could stay in the honeymoon suite at the Brown Palace. If he didn't hurry, she might be spending her honeymoon with Mr. Hollywood. He should have grabbed Vi when he saw her with her hair down and kissed her with all the love that he'd been saving up for years. What was he thinking? He was thinking of himself.

Jenky and Caesar took a short cut back to the boarding house. They passed in front of a respectable tavern where a barkeep was adjusting a poster in the window. Sweet summer days and a cool McDoull's the caption read. The illustration was of a beautiful woman lying on a bed of buttercups with one shoulder of her dress pulled down. An overflowing mug of beer was superimposed on it. Her smile was familiar, fetching, and carefree. Jenky paused to look again. If he didn't know better, he would say the model on the poster was Violet Hendricks. His face went red.

～

Violet waved as Reg drove off on his desert adventure. She still tasted his cigarettes. His kisses were exciting and she relished them, but those doggone cigarettes took the longest to disappear from his breath. She had considered slipping a pack of Dentyne gum into his camera case. Right now all she wanted was to brush her teeth.

It had been a while since she'd had the place to herself. Violet pulled on her rubber boots and went straight to the windmill pump with her tin cup, toothbrush, and powder. She took the milking stool from the barn and sat brushing and rinsing until there was no grit on her teeth from the powder and no taste of cigarettes in her mouth. She cupped her hand and drank the cool water several times before it spilled out on the dirt. She looked around at the refreshed trees and plants. It was good to know that the earth was no longer parched and her beans, if they hadn't washed away, would soon break through the soil to grow in the sun. She tilted her chin upward, closed her eyes, and whispered, "Thank you."

～

That night Violet and Bean sat on the porch listening to the frogs and crickets until the mosquitoes got the better of her. The two pals went inside and she reread the Superman story for the tenth time. She needed her own man of steel to love her and make her miss him when he was away, like now. How did a girl know when her heart was leaning towards love if she didn't long for him?

Violet turned out her lamp and lay watching the moonlit scene outside her window. An owl hooted somewhere along the creek. Would she ever share this kind of bedroom moonlight with a husband? She didn't know if her dear Jenky actually loved her or if he was destined to be a bachelor politician. And Reg could be a bad prospect, too. He was a traveling man who drank a lot and was allergic to farm life and never let her see past his flirtatious self—except for sharing the piglets story. She giggled to think about baby pigs licking ice cream out of his golden curls.

～

After checking her fields for washouts, Violet made a list of extra chores and little projects that needed her attention:

1. tighten clothesline wire
2. check wicks under water trough in chicken house
3. replace posts on both sides of culvert
4. clean culvert
5. write a friendly note to Jenky in Denver

She pinned the list to the curtain on her kitchen window and turned back to the table. Normally, this was her lunch time, after the morning chores and initial crop-tending were done. But she wasn't at all hungry today. In fact, her stomach burned, churned, and seemed to creep up into her throat with a vengeance. The room shifted and tilted. It was just about then that Violet got sicker than a mule. Sicker than she had ever been in her life.

Tyrel bounced around in his mail truck. The storm had made his deliveries twice as much trouble. He had been pulled out of ditches and mudslides a dozen times by friendly farmers perched on their muddy tractors. The sunshine brought easier travels though. He chugged along, viewing the nasty mess that had slipped into Violet's cow pasture from King's farm on the hill above and now had gradually oozed its way towards her outbuildings.

"Dang. That's a whole lot of pig dung. Bet it stinks up her place." He turned in at Violet's. "Hey, Peaches, I got a packet for you," he yelled and waited for her to respond. Her Maxwell and Farmall were both parked near the barn. "Vi-o-let...come out, come out, wherever you are." No response. Tyrel beeped his horn, then walked to the back door and knocked. He turned the knob and laid her packet on the table. Bean came right to him and meowed. He bent down to pet the cat and that's when he saw Violet on the floor in the parlor.

Jenky answered the phone in his office at the Capitol Building. The connection was not good. "I'm sorry. Who is this again?"

"It's me, Ethel," the caller said.

Jenky jumped up. "What's happened? Is Violet all right?"

"No, son. She is real sick. Tyrel found her passed out and went for help. Glenn and Bessie Stanley took her into Cortez. Jim is taking care of her animals as long as she needs him to."

His eyes burned with tears. "What are her symptoms and is she conscious?"

"I don't know, Jenky. She had been throwing up when Tyrel found her. Howard says it sure reminds him of the cholera in the Great War."

"How could Violet have gotten cholera? I'm coming home," he said and reached for his hat. He fastened Caesar's leash, turned off the lights, and locked the door.

~

Jenky drove all night on a different route through Utah. He knew there was serious roadwork on Wolf Creek Pass. He arrived in Dove Creek and called the doctor's office in Cortez. The nurse assured him that they were taking care of her as best they could, but she was not responding. Dr. Warren had given her a diagnosis of *gastroenteritis* and said it was crucial for her to drink fluids. In case Violet's illness was bacterial, he had also given her a dose of sulfa.

"Is she conscious?" Jenky asked.

"Off and on," the nurse said, "but she has a high fever that interferes with her thinking. We understand that she has no family. Are you a friend?"

"Yes, and I would like to visit her."

"No, no. She is not ready for visitors."

"I can get her to drink." He had absolutely nothing upon which to base such a statement.

The nurse was interested. "Then, by all means, come as soon as you can."

~

He left Caesar with Ethel and, despite the muddy dirt road, was there within an hour, thinking the whole time of ways to approach Violet's situation. The hospital consisted of ten beds housed in two cottages that the genial Dr. Warren had connected with an office and waiting area. A sturdy, middle-aged nurse led him to her room, speaking softly about Violet's muscle cramps and her heart rate and blood pressure being low. He didn't dare look towards the bed yet. He was shown the water pitcher and drinking glass.

"It's sugar water with a little salt in it," the nurse explained. She's not out of the woods yet. Keep the ice bag on her forehead to help with the fever. I'm only down the hall but I'll be back to take her vitals. Dr. Warren is on a house call, delivering a breech baby, but he'll be in afterward. We have to get more fluids down her. Better say a prayer." The nurse closed the door behind her.

Jenky filled a glass halfway with the sugar water and turned back to Violet. He gasped at how this battle had ravaged his beautiful girl. He couldn't allow himself to lose his emotions over her symptoms. It was the battle inside her that must be his focus. He pulled a stool next to the bed and touched her hot cheek.

"Can you hear me, Vi?" he whispered. She made a whimpering sound, making his heart hurt. "It's me."

"Papa?" she whispered.

His thoughts ran ahead of his mouth, for once. "Yes, Vi, I want you to sip this water. You are very sick and water will make you better." He lifted her head and held the glass to her cracked lips. Jenky tipped the glass and the water ran down her chin and onto the pillow. She coughed.

"I can't, Papa."

"It'll be a chore, but you are a hard worker." He leaned in close to her ear. "Nobody thinks you can drink this water. They say you aren't tough enough, but I know better. Try again, sweet girl," Jenky said as tears blurred his vision. He blinked and held the glass to her mouth again. Her lips trembled as she worked to control them. "You can do anything, Vi. Look what…" His voice broke. "Look what you've done with the farm all by yourself."

He watched as she took in a small amount of the liquid. "Gotta swallow now; get the water down to your tummy. That's my girl. Here's one more, then we'll wait a while."

He lowered her back to the pillow but kept his hand underneath her head in case she gagged. Violet looked right through him. The dark circles under her eyes rattled Jenky. Her stomach growled like a mountain lion and he thought she might throw up but she stared at him instead. He never realized how fragile she really was. An avalanche of guilt seized him as he considered all the years that had passed without them being man and wife. Now she might join the angels and they would never have shared the joy of being together. He prayed.

Violet closed her eyes, putting Jenky in a panic. "Time for more water, Vi. Show everybody that you are one tough lady. Give it another try." She stirred and opened her mouth. At least she wasn't dead. He lifted her head and tilted the glass and she swallowed. They repeated the process until the nurse knocked on the door.

"Any luck?" she asked, pumping up the blood pressure cuff.

"A little. Does she ever open her eyes and stare at you?"

The nurse nodded as she listened to Violet's heart. She took the stethoscope out of her ears. "Bless her. She is out of her head. Would you excuse us for a while? There are chairs in the reception room."

Jenky wandered into the waiting room and dropped into a chair. Other folks sat around also, waiting quietly or reading as they worried about their loved ones. This was the only hospital for miles. He bent forward and rested his head in his hands. Only a fool would have wasted years of longing and loneliness for the sake of stubborn bashfulness—where emotions were concerned. The Devil was laughing at him every Christmas when he sent out his solitary card to Violet. He should have walked over to her house the morning after the hayride and asked Nev for his daughter's hand. How she must have bitten her tongue to keep from chewing him out every summer. Caesar had more sense than his master.

∼

Dr. Warren entered the waiting room in his laboratory coat. He was a tall, thin man with silver hair, a trimmed moustache and beard. Today he was not his usual jovial self. "Jenkins, sorry to meet under the circumstances," he said embracing Jenky. "Come down the hallway a bit. We've got ourselves one sick young lady in there. Any ideas as to how this came about?"

Jenky was taken aback that the doctor might be aware of his potential relationship, if any, to Violet. They stopped near Violet's room.

"Well? Don't look at me like that, Jenkins, everybody in Dolores and Montezuma County knows that you two are star-crossed lovers. What would she be doing to have gotten this sick?"

Star-crossed lovers? Jenky couldn't look at the doctor who had cared for the Butler family since they had moved to the area. "I'm not sure, Doctor. Would it help to try and find out or should I stay around and get her to drink the sugar and salt water?"

The doctor looked at Violet's chart. "I see that you've helped us out with that already. Stick around for a while and get that gal hydrated. When you get back out to Dove Creek, do a little detective work and let me know if anything is unusual. Check out Violet's place. Oh, and bring me a sample of her drinking water. I want to be sure of the treatment. We don't have a big lab here and by the time I send a sample off, our patient could be…we could possibly lose her. I do have a microscope."

Jenky's eyes went straight to the doctor's. "I'll get started on the hydration," he said and knocked on Violet's door.

y the time Jenky had left the hospital, Violet had been sipping water off and on for four hours. Her vital signs were somewhat better, but she still had fever and was dazed and confused. Jenky was weary but not confused about his mission. He told what he knew at Sitton's. Ethel had written a prayer request on the big bulletin board. Jenky inhaled a sandwich and washed it down with coffee before putting Caesar in the pickup and taking off for the Hendricks farm. He hoped Regal Reggie wasn't around. As Jenky maneuvered his way through the muddy potholes, Caesar kept his head out the window. On approaching the turn-in, he was relieved to see that the Roadster was gone. Jenky parked next to the Maxwell and got out.

The animals were quiet, as if they knew their mistress was not home and all was not well. Bean came right out to greet them, rubbing noses with Caesar and purring as Jenky scooped him up in his arms. He walked around the barn and peeked in the tack room. Reggie had a few things still there, but he must have gone somewhere with his photo equipment. Jenky made a loop around the house before going inside. There was a large envelope addressed to Violet on the table. Bean jumped down as Jenky checked inside the empty ice box. He emptied the drip pan outside the door, and then inspected the pantry. There was a plate of rock-hard biscuits, but no other suspect food. He crumbled them in his hands and pitched them out the door for the chickens. The dishes were all put away and everything was tidy. He looked through her kitchen window as she must do every day but turned away from the sadness of that thought. He spied her list of things to do pinned to the curtain and read the last entry with tears stinging his eyes. He put it in his pocket.

He checked the parlor, that still held the smell of sickness, then stood sadly by her Sears kit house plans and the modern bathroom illustration, which were neatly pinned to the wall. He ducked his head and peeked into the side room which had served as her bedroom until Nev passed away. The furniture had been moved to the tack room to accommodate her infamous boarder.

Last of all, he dared to enter Violet's bedroom. Her bed had been hastily made, probably by Glenn's wife. There were no contaminated bedtime snacks left on her lamp table—only the Sears Catalog, her Bible, and a comic book. Jenky gently opened the wardrobe door, not hoping for clues about her illness, but only to be near her things. The black dress and purple duster hung next to one of the shirts he had given her. The old-fashioned black oxfords were placed neatly next to a pair of her new overalls. Melancholy overwhelmed him as he closed the door and sank to the foot of her bed.

Jenky ached for her presence. His shame lay heavy against his heart. For all her sassiness and spunk, Violet's life was composed of dawn to dusk hard labor and solitude. Yet simplicity, loyalty, frugality and dreams of a beautiful future had shaped her too. It wasn't fair. His life was easy and always had been. He spent his days reading, writing, and forging compromises. He could choose to be alone or engage in hearty fellowship at his whim. The future for him was about legislative deadlines and taking monetary risks with his bank accounts full of money because he never bought anything.

Her future was pinned to the wall and yet she had never left this old farm. She had clung to her dreams and they might have, at one time, included him. What was he thinking all those years? He had been a smug, selfish jerk and did not deserve Violet's love. It was so like him to go over and over his emotional history towards Vi without altering the future in a positive way. He would quickly recognize that in another person, but never in himself.

Jenky blew out his breath and pulled himself up. He ran his hand over her old blue bedspread. He remembered it from decades ago when her mother, Alice Ann, had ordered it from the catalog and shown his mother the illustration. Now Violet slept under it, all alone. Jenky let the tears roll freely down his face. He couldn't take it if he lost her, especially now that he could see their lives for what they were, and for what they could have been. In that moment, a flaming desire to turn everything inside out, upside down, and sideways until all of Violet's dreams could come true, consumed him. He would make it happen, even if he was no longer part of those dreams.

~

Bean and Caesar played tug of war with their new favorite toy, an old mop head, while Jenky got a water sample from the hand pump by the windmill. He caught the water in an empty jam jar and set it in the pickup seat. The air was not sweet with honeysuckle as it normally was in the early summer. Instead, it was extra heavy with the pungent smell of swine manure.

He went to the truck, put on his rubber fishing boots, and schlepped his way along the vegetable patch acreage that Violet always planted for home use. A few sprouts were punching their way through the soil, but much of the area was standing in foul-smelling water. Jenky shaded his eyes and followed the path of what seemed to be alien, rocky soil up the hill to a big patch of exposed fence posts that had broken off from King's pig farm.

"Oh my gosh." He hurried back to the pickup to put on his regular shoes, leaving his putrid-smelling boots in a heap behind the barn. He would buy new ones.

Jenky leaned against his pickup, considering the impact of the mudslide, the smell of it, and the fact that Violet's water source was from an old, hand-dug well that was probably shallow. A shallow well could be more vulnerable for contamination by surface water from a storm, especially if the storm water carried runoff from a contaminated source—such as manure from a pig farm. It made sense to Jenky that Violet had ingested the culprit water from her pump. A lab test on the water in the jam jar would prove his theory.

Before Jenky and Caesar drove back to Cortez with the water specimen, he checked Violet's tool box in the barn and found a heavy-duty pair of pliers. He went straight to her clothesline and tightened it at both ends. On his way back to the pickup, he stopped in the henhouse, got down on his knees and checked the wicks in the water trough heaters. He would buy new ones tomorrow. Heck, he would buy a whole new trough and feeders so she'd have them before cold autumn nights returned.

At the hospital, Jenky parked under a big cottonwood. He went inside to fill Caesar's water bowl with fresh water and put it next to him under the tree. "Stay." He patted his head. "Good boy."

Dr. Warren gave him the report. "Your theory is supported by my microscope, so now we know what we are dealing with, at least. She still has fever and confusion, but is taking fluids. You can see her if you like. Keep up the good work with the water." He returned to his office.

Jenky moved slowly down the hallway. His lack of sleep was beginning to wear him down.

Violet's eyes were closed, but she didn't seem as gaunt as earlier in the day. He poured water into the glass and moved the stool next to the bed.

"Time for a drink, Vi," he said, slipping his hand under her head. "Can you hear me?" Her eyes fluttered open but closed again. Jenky lifted her head gently. "Here comes the water. You can almost taste it." He let a tiny amount drip onto her lips and, as she became aware of the moisture, he gave her more to drink and swallow.

Jenky sat with her, repeating the feeding, until he fell asleep on the job with his head resting on the side of the bed.

"Time to go home, sir." The nurse woke him with a nudge. "I'll take good care of her."

Jenky widened his eyes and checked on Violet. "I think her temperature is coming down."

The nurse nodded. "Can you drive home?"

He rubbed his stubbly face. "I'll be okay. I need to take care of some business for Violet tomorrow. I'll call to see if she is still on the upswing. Is there coffee anywhere?"

She smiled. "I'll make you some. We don't want you running off the road tonight." She went down the hall.

Jenky exhaled and mumbled, "No. I have too many things to do to sleep in a ditch." He thought seriously about kissing Violet's cheek, but it didn't seem right to do that while she was even the least bit delirious. No, better to get on with his work.

He was back in Cortez the next morning. He ate breakfast at the local diner, then went to the lumberyard, the big hardware store, and paid a visit to a well drilling business. Then, last of all, he made the arduous drive to Rico, the mountainous county seat of Dolores County. He drank coffee and a hot meal after visiting the courthouse.

It was dusk when Jenky pulled into King's junkyard. He got out and was encircled by barking dogs and flies. King came to the door.

"Shut up!" King was in his skivvies. "Jenkins Butler, is that you?"

"Hello, King." Jenky waited at the bottom step.

King came out and joined him. "What can I do for you? I saw the prayer request for Violet. I'm sure sorry."

"Thank you. I surely could use your help, King. There's a problem with Vi's water well that's made her really sick."

King scratched his behind. "I used to know about wells, Jenky, but that's left me now."

"Here's what happened. That big storm chipped off part of your feed lot and washed it down into Vi's well water. My idea is to move your feed lot to the other pasture and put new topsoil and grass seed on the old one. I'll help you do it and pay for the seed and pay you for your time and trouble."

King's brow knitted. "Folks are praying for Violet 'cause of me?" He bent over, covered his face, and began to moan.

"No, King." Jenky patted his back. "Folks are praying because she's in the hospital. It was nothing anybody could have predicted."

King straightened up, cackled, and clapped his hands. Jenky wasn't sure what to do next until King stopped and pointed at him.

"You, Representative Jenky Butler, would get out there in hog muck and help me move my porkers to another feed lot?"

Jenky nodded. "And put down seed and topsoil as well as pay you cash. I do know how to work."

King shut one eye. "When?"

"Tomorrow?"

"Why the hurry?"

"I want to take care of the problem up here while a crew from Cortez drills a new well at the Hendricks's place. I got the permit today."

King put out a grimy hand. "Deal."

Jenky shook on it. "One more thing. I don't want this to get around. This is personal between you and me. I'm doing it for Violet."

"Moving hogs to a feedlot ain't too romantic, Jenky. That's always been your problem with her. I can give you advice about women while we work. Better get here early before them boogers eat. They'll follow the food. Bring a kerchief to put over your nose. Better dab some fancy, smell-um-good on it, too." He cackled again then stopped. "You a praying man?"

"I'm praying for Vi."

"Naw, I figured that. Need to pray that the wind blows in the morning." King laughed again and saluted Jenky as he drove away.

~

The next morning, Jenky left Caesar at home. The eastern horizon hinted at pink and orange. He had a thermos of coffee, a bandana scarf, his new fishing waders, shovels, and grass seed he'd bought for his own backyard from Sitton's. He turned in at Violet's and fed Bean. Jim would be there soon to feed the cows and chickens and do the milking, if needed.

He moved along the road at a thinking speed. He would take a break and call from Sitton's to check on Violet. If she was doing better, he would hang around her place while the drilling crew was there. He had plenty to accomplish before she came home. He prayed she was improving. He forgot to pray for the wind to be blowing while they worked. Poor old King. Jenky's father had told him that King had horrific shell shock in the Great War. That would certainly account for his strange behavior.

～

Jenky put on his waders, tied the red bandana around his neck, and pulled on his gloves at King's place. The dogs barked, but they appeared to be shut up in a shed. He knocked on King's door several times, but then decided to check out back. He shouted for him, but all he heard back was the dogs. The place smelled rancid. Each breath burned his throat. He called King's name again.

"Yo, Senator!" King yelled. "Over here. Walk slow."

Jenky walked through a sea of grunting pigs, many of whom were still resting. He could barely make out King's location in the shimmering glow of dawn. King had several bales of hay and was busy spreading them over the ground.

Jenky had been holding his breath. He let it out with his words. "Good morning."

"Mornin'. You want to help spread this hay? I found some banners in my trash collection that we can tie to the fence. Pigs are curious. They'll want to see what's going on." King stood up straight. "I see you're prepared. You don't want to scare pigs, so move real slow. They can't see too good but I think if I can get a few to head this way, others will follow. We are gonna do some lifting. You got a good back?"

The odor was about to make Jenky throw up as he finished spreading the hay. "My back is fine. What are we lifting?"

"Slop troughs. Don't worry, they are empty, but I've got buckets of slop ready to go." King chuckled and looked around. "I think it's as good a time as any. Let's go. Pull that kerchief up like a bandit."

They moved eight troughs while the pigs watched. Jenky recognized one big boar as the charming hog Caesar had herded, and who had chased Reggie up the hill to Violet's. He was the first to investigate the activity when King called the pigs to breakfast. While Jenky poured the vile slop into the troughs, King went back to encourage the pigs to move. They came quietly, almost eerily to the new feeding area. Jenky was amazed at their soft snorts and composure.

King left the gate partially open. "There are some pig-headed stragglers, but they'll come when they get hungry. Just like politicians, eh? There's good shade under the cottonwood over there and, come winter, I'll have a shed for the survivors. You wanna help at killing time?"

Jenky shuddered. "No thanks. I'll leave that to the experts. I don't see how you do this alone."

"I got a couple of good-for-nothings that help out at killing time. You did all right for a politician." King slapped Jenky on the back. "I may have to vote for you again."

"Are we ready to work on the old feed lot now?" Jenky asked.

King laughed. "I'll let old Mr. Sun dry up the place some first, then the good-for-nothings can clean it up and scatter seed around."

Jenky was elated that he didn't have to stay. "I have the seed in the truck. I'll get it." He took off for the pickup.

King lumbered behind. "I sure do like your kerchief, Senator. How come you didn't use it to cover your nose?"

Jenky hefted the bag out of the pickup bed. "The smell wasn't too bad." Actually, he had forgotten about the bandana. "Here, you can have it and these waders, too." He held the bandana out to King. "And here are twenty dollar bills for your trouble. I appreciate your cooperation."

King tied the bandana around his head like a band. "You don't owe me nothing, Jenky. It was fun to see a politician toting pig troughs." He hooked his thumbs under his overall straps and did his rendition of a pompous politician walking in circle. Then he exploded into a guffaw.

Jenky laughed too. "I insist. If you don't take the money, I'll be offended. By the way, I'm a member of the Colorado House of Representatives at the General Assembly in Denver. I'm not any kind of senator. Just call me Jenky."

King wobbled his head. "How 'bout I stick with Politician Butler? I ain't takin' your money. *Now git*—before you pass out." He laughed all the way to the shed, but then took a few steps back. "You watch out for that yellow headed fancy dancer. He's up to no good with Violet." He saluted, and then opened the shed door to let his dogs out.

Jenky took off the gloves and waders and pitched them towards King's windmill to let him decide whether to wash them or not. Jenky's jaw was set as he started the truck and drove off with his head out the window, breathing fresh air.

~

He called the hospital with Ethel at his elbow. Jenky could tell that Ethel smelled pig on him, but she didn't mention it.

The nurse answered and had encouraging news. "She is coming around and very curious about how this all happened. I bet you are sure anxious to see her. You might want to wait until this evening. I am going to give her a bath and wash her hair."

"Thanks for doing that. She'll feel better."

"All in a day's work. Call anytime."

Jenky hung up. "Did you hear the news?"

Ethel chuckled. "She's a loud one. I'm so thankful that Violet is better. I'll post it on the board right now. Wonder what caused her to get sick."

"It was her water well," Jenky said, deciding to confide. "The storm brought some bad runoff water from animals."

"You don't say. King's pigs, I'm sure. That poor child. Thank goodness for sulfa."

"Amen. I'll be back later to call again. Thanks, Ethel. By the way, here's a list of groceries I want to get for Violet when she comes home. I'll put you in charge of that."

Ethel wrote the news in big letters. She watched Jenky's blue truck drive away. She shook her head. "High time you woke up, Jenkins Butler, to your true feelings about our Violet." She pinned the update about Violet right next to a news story about the increasing numbers of Jewish refugees fleeing persecution in Europe by the Nazis.

~

A red and yellow bird with black wings landed on Violet's window sill. It peered in the window, tipping its head from side to side before flying away. It pleased Violet to see nature once again.

The nurse saw it too as she brought in fresh water. "That was a Western Tanager, male of course. So colorful." She fluffed Violet's pillow. "I'm a birdwatcher as you might tell. The mister and me didn't have kids, so we took up a hobby together. My name's Annie."

Violet smiled. "Good to meet you, Annie. Do you know when I might be released? I have a farm to run."

"Dr. Warren says that you will be here a few more days. You were one sick girl. If the Butler boy hadn't gotten sugar water down you, we wouldn't be having this conversation."

Violet raised her head off the pillow. "Jenky was here?"

"Sure was. He looked like the dickens but he was the one who kept you from the grave. I think he's coming back this evening."

Violet frowned. "I don't want him to see me like this."

Annie laughed. "Good thing you didn't have a mirror when he was here before. You have improved considerably since then. Are you hungry? Let's see how some chicken broth goes down. We have some warming in the kitchen. I'll be right back."

Violet had stopped listening. Jenky was in Denver; she was sure of it. But there was only one Butler boy that everybody knew because he was their state representative. Gosh. She must have been deathly sick and she still didn't feel like getting out of bed. Jenky had seen her looking worse. Like when they had to push his car out of a muddy ditch in high school and got sprayed with mud or when they went camping with their dads and she fell in the river and had to wear her papa's skivvies for the rest of the day.

It wasn't as though Reg was coming to see her. He expected glamour. She wasn't sure what Jenky expected.

∼

On his way to Violet's home, Jenky prioritized his mental list. Number one was to get a new water source for her. Number two was to clean out the culvert and replace the posts that washed out. Number three was to keep these projects as quiet as possible. It was his business if he helped Violet through this and he didn't want silly gossip floating around regarding his reasons.

As he approached Violet's, he could see the drilling rig and crew hard at work. He also saw Tyrel's mail truck parked next to the barn. At least Reg's Roadster wasn't there. Jenky exhaled. Tyrel was the worst gossip in Dolores County, and he had arrived earlier on this particular mail route than ever before.

The drilling rig was extremely noisy, so nobody noticed Jenky's arrival. He walked up next to Tyrel and put an arm around his shoulders. Tyrel dropped the cigarette right out of his mouth and hollered liked he'd been bitten by a rattler.

"Sorry," Jenky said, laughing. "I thought you heard me pull in."

Tyrel dusted off his cigarette but decided to put it out. "You almost stopped my ticker. It's real swell of you to do this for Violet. I figure it was most likely the hog muck that washed down from King's feedlot that got into that old well of hers. I suppose you know that I'm the one who found her. She had puked all over herself. She would've died if it weren't for me." He grinned like a donkey.

"And we all appreciate that, Tyrel. Aren't you running our route early today?"

"Yeah. I saw the rig going through town and thought I'd switch things up a little, you know, see what was going on. How's Violet? Wonder if her boarder has skipped out on his rent? Did you just come from Cortez?" He raised his brow. "Steal a kiss or two in the hospital?"

Oh, boy. "Listen, Tyrel, if you're on a break, would you mind helping me move firewood from the barn to her back porch bin? The one on the front porch is already loaded. I also could use your help unloading new feeders and water troughs."

When he was cornered, Tyrel had an odd habit of drawing his tongue down over his prominent front teeth to make a popping sound, as he was doing now. "Well…pop, pop, pop…I'd give anything to help with that, but duty calls. You know our motto, *Snow, rain, a hot day, not even a dark night can stop us from puttin' the mail out*," he said and popped his tongue again.

Jenky chuckled at Tyrel's version of the motto and watched as Tyrel went to the mail truck and turned left at the county road, to finish the route.

The well-driller and his son were busy, so Jenky went straight to the house to check on Bean. He found him under the front porch, wide-eyed and frightened of the commotion. Jenky put him inside and filled his water dish. Bean curled up in the rocking chair. Jenky set the feeders and troughs in the barn for later.

He backed up to the culvert and unloaded the posts. Tyrel wouldn't return this way because this route took him on a loop and then he had the other routes to complete. Jenky unloaded a rake and shovel and went to work on the debris in the culvert. Surely he had the skills to accomplish this job. There was a considerable amount of mud, dead plants, a rat, and few pieces of trash. He even found a shoe. The drudgery gave him more time to think, something in which he excelled.

He had seriously considered plumbing the house for Violet as a surprise, but something in his head told him to ask her first. There might not be enough time anyway. He should pick roses from his mother's garden and have them on every table when she came home. It might take that sick smell out of the place, too. Were roses blooming yet? When the drillers finished, he would open up the house during the daytime. Fresh air was always in season.

Next up was replacing the fence posts. He had helped with fencing before, but this time the posts weren't connected. They were the end posts on either side of the lane near the culvert. He would have to do a bang-up job or they would look like a child had installed them. Seems like there should be more support at the end, but he wasn't sure. He examined the ruined posts which were both rotted off at ground level.

"Where did you get those politician posts?" someone said behind him.

Jenky turned to find King laughing and still wearing the bandana around his head. He was also wearing the discarded waders. "Hello, King. Did you walk here?"

King turned his head to spit and wiped his mouth on his sleeve. "Yeah. I wanted to see what happened with the mudslide. It was bad, huh? I'm wearing your rubber boot britches. Hope that's okay. What is it you are hoping to do with those sissy posts?"

Jenky had to laugh. "You can have the waders. I'm trying to replace these end posts that washed out with the storm."

King hooted. "Well, your new ones are all wrong. You need cut posts from a cedar tree. I've got some at my place. "It would be an embarrassment to the county if you were to put in what you've got there. Take me home and I'll give you a couple."

"I'll take you home and give you twenty dollars. Then would you put them in for me?"

"You're dying to give me them dollar bills. I'll take two of 'em off your hands for the posts and I'll put the dang things in to save your hide from Violet's torment. She's a frisky little thing. You planning to marry her?"

He turned red. "I appreciate your offer, King. Go ahead and take my truck. I'll put these posts back in the barn. You need anything else?"

"Nah. Leave 'em. I'll use them to shore up the posts." He tapped Jenky's arm. "You need to shore yourself up. Women don't ask men to marry them, even a spirited one like Violet. If you ain't got the guts to ask her, you ain't got what it takes to keep her. I had my day with a woman like that. She was a honey but she got away. Folks may think I'm crazy, but I know about the ladies." He gave a wolf whistle and rolled his eyes.

"Ladies like to be surprised by a lover man."

Jenky shook with laughter. "I know you're right, and I am working on it. Thanks for the advice." He stood by as King got in his tidy truck wearing the filthy waders. He was so excited that he forgot to give his signature salute. Maybe this wasn't such a fine idea, but at least he wouldn't have to smell the hog farm. On second thought, yes, he would be smelling the hog farm after King drove his truck twice, wearing muck-encrusted waders. Powerful thinking, Rep. Butler.

The well men were eating lunch when Jenky walked up to the house. "How's it coming along?" he asked.

The older man shook hands with him. "Going fine. No problems."

"How much longer?"

The man took off his hat and scratched his head. "We should be out of here in a couple of days at the latest, at best—tomorrow."

"Good. Thanks for your hard work," Jenky said, "and for rearranging your schedule."

The man grinned. "You betcha. You'll get the bill for it, son."

"That's fine. It's an emergency."

Violet shuffled to the bathroom with Annie. She saw her face in the mirror. Jenky would be here within an hour. There was no time to improve her pale, drawn face. Her hair was down, too, but not in an attractive way. Annie could braid it for her.

Jenky came in the door with daffodils from his mother's garden. He had bathed, shaved, and slicked back his hair.

Violet was propped up with pillows. She had bitten her chapped lips and pinched her cheeks for color. Annie, not understanding her assignment properly, had braided her hair in two braids, like a little school girl.

"Hi," Violet said, her heart pumping faster than it had in days.

Jenky raked up his courage. "There's my girl," he said and, without warning, kissed her forehead.

Now the color came naturally to her cheeks. "I like the flowers. Thanks."

He kept holding them. "I like your hair. I remember when you wore it that way every day. Are you feeling stronger?"

She sighed. "Not much. The doctor said it would take time. I thought you were in Denver."

Don't chicken out. "I was, but it was time to come back." *Cluck, cluck, cluck.* "Actually, I…"

"Doctor Warren said that bacteria got into my drinking water and made me sick. He said it was probably carried there by the storm. I'll have to get my well cleaned out or something."

Annie came in and put the daffodils in a vase. She could see there was something going on between the two, so she made a quick exit.

"I hope you don't mind, Vi, but I am taking care of that for you."

"What do you mean? You are cleaning the well for me?"

Jenky was still standing, holding his hat. "No. It's contaminated. The well is too shallow anyway, and when a big storm like we had, comes through, runoff water seeps into it."

"What am I supposed to do?"

He fiddled with his hat. "Vi, I hired a well driller to dig you a deep well. He should be done by the time you are discharged." He didn't know if she was going to thank him or rise up out of the hospital bed and beat on him with a pillow.

She blinked a few times. He could see the gears turning, then she said, "Thank you, Jenky. I will find a way to pay you back. That was generous of you."

Whew. "I wanted to help. I came as soon…"

"Where is the new well?"

"Just east of the house, closer than the old one. It'll be easy to access for plumbing, too."

Violet looked away. "I'll never be able to afford that."

Jenky sat on the stool and moved it closer to the bed. "If you'll let me, I can have plumbers out there by next week. You could have running water indoors by next month or so."

She turned to him. "Why would you want to do that?"

"Because I care about you, Vi." He fiddled with his hat. "We go back a long way. Why should I have indoor plumbing and you have to haul water? You work hard enough as it is." *Cluck, cluck, cluck.*

"Is that all?" she asked quietly, taking his hat away and trying to look him in the eye.

He met her gaze. "Of course not."

"Talk to me, Jenky." She held out her hand.

He took it. "I wrote you a letter but it's at home."

"Is it a Christmas card?"

"No. It's real."

"Can't you tell me to my face what's written in the card?"

He cleared his throat. "You are the best person I've ever known, Vi. You are beautiful, smart, and funny." He watched for her reaction. "And nobody could ever mean as much to me. I want us to be together." As soon as he saw the tears in her eyes, he shut up. "I'm sorry. What can I do?"

"Kiss me, please. I..."

With the worst possible timing ever, the door opened and Dr. Warren came in with Annie. "Hello, Jenkins. What do you think about our patient?"

Jenky jumped like a school boy caught putting a frog in the teacher's desk. "She looks great."

Annie moved Jenky's hat off the bed and began taking Violet's blood pressure.

Dr. Warren scanned his clipboard. "Her blood pressure is stabilizing. Good, good. I'm glad we jumped right on that low potassium level. Dehydration can do that. We are keeping her on the sulfa though because she was dealing with some nasty stuff on different levels." He wrote notes on the clipboard as the nurse tidied the room.

"How do you like her braids?" Annie asked. "She looks like a school girl."

Jenky caught Violet's eye and smiled. "Yes, she does."

The doctor put his clipboard down. "You'll have to give us a bit of privacy now, Jenkins. I want to make sure she is ready to go home, as early as tomorrow after lunch. Will you be the one to pick her up?"

"Yes sir. It will be a privilege. I should probably get on the road now but I'm about out of gas. Hope somebody is open. I'll see you tomorrow, Violet." He smiled longingly at her.

Violet returned it with the same sentiment.

The next morning, Jenky clipped the best tulips and daffodils from the garden and put them in a bucket of water covered with a wet pillowcase. He carefully tucked some of his mother's nicest vases into a box and started the truck. Caesar sat on the porch, whining.

"You can go with me tomorrow, boy. The well will be finished by then." Jenky backed the car onto the driveway and sang out the window, "Vi's coming home today." He had not slept much for thinking about their conversation the night before. He had the letter in his pocket and a plan in his head. He whistled all the way to her house.

His first stop was to see the posts that King had set. They looked first-rate to him. Never judge a man by his appearance. His father had taught Jenky that old adage, and King had proven it. Vi was coming home today. Thank God.

He parked his truck by the barn so he wouldn't be in the way of the drilling equipment. He dragged out the old ones and set up the new chicken feeders and watering troughs. All was in order. He knew nothing about well drilling, but things seemed to be coming to a close there. He carried the bucket of flowers into the house and opened all the windows. Then he brought in the vases, fed Bean, and dumped out the cat box. He refilled it with dirt he'd brought from his yard. The wood bin was full as was the camping water cooler that he had set up in the kitchen. Now all he needed was to get ice from Cahone for her icebox. He would stop at Sitton's for groceries to fill it, including Coca-Cola, her favorite drink. Clara and Bessie Stanley, as well as several other ladies, were sending over food every day for ten days.

He whistled around Violet's house, considering the best place to put his letter. He wanted it to be private reading but fun for her to discover. What would be the first thing she would do when she came home? Probably go to bed. He should have changed her sheets since she'd been sick. She might have an extra set. He looked around but found none. He could buy a new set at Sitton's on his way back from the ice house.

~

Jenky walked in the store with a big grin. "Good morning, Ethel. Today's the day!"

"I know," she said with a big smile and raised shoulders. "It's so wonderful. I have all your groceries boxed up and ready to go except for the cold items. I'll get those right away. There are a few extra special treats for Violet from Howard and me. Anything thing else you can think of?"

"Yes. Don't you agree that it would make her happy to have fresh linens on her bed? I'm sure they haven't been changed since she first came down with this sickness. I couldn't find an extra set anywhere."

Ethel smiled at his thoughtfulness. "Violet would never spend a dime on anything that wasn't necessary. Except for her Cokes." She led the way to the linens shelves. "Here's one. It has a little touch of blue piping on the hems. I assume you want the whole set."

"Of course. Would it be too personal to buy her a new terry cloth towel? The one she has must have been her grandpa's."

"Definitely too personal." Ethel winked. "I won't breathe a word to anyone, Jenky. She deserves every good thing. I have a thick white one right here and it'll be our secret."

Ethel wrapped the linens in brown paper. As she taped the last one, Pauline came to the register.

"Mr. Butler," Pauline said, "there's a phone call for you."

Ethel and Jenky looked at one another as he went to the phone. Anxiety gave him a shaky voice. "Hello? Jenky Butler here."

"Jenky. It's Ralph Carr. I'm in Durango for a conference right now at the Strater Hotel. We have several topics on the agenda and one of them is the great Rural Electric Association and its upcoming progress in your district. I know it's short notice, Jenky, but this is a golden opportunity to be the voice of your constituents. I suggest that you meet with us. We are about to have lunch and a speaker, but you are only an hour or two away, right?"

He didn't know what to say. After all, it was the Governor calling. Two hours over, two hours in Durango, and two hours back. Dang. Of all days.

"Jenky? You still there?" the Governor asked.

"Yes, sir. Let me iron out a few personal commitments and I'll be over."

"Good. That's what I wanted to hear. Sorry to call you at the last minute, but we couldn't find a phone number for you anywhere this past week. I thought you were still in your office. Your next pet project should be getting phone service over there in the Four Corners. I'll see you sooner than later then. No telling how long this speaker will take. Big windbag from Houston talking about oil." He clicked off.

Jenky hung up and ran his fingers through his hair. He would have to explain this to Violet somehow. He wanted to be with her when she was dismissed. He wanted to be the one to drive her home and talk all the way. He wanted to carry her into her house. He wanted to bring electricity to her little house. He wanted to bring her to his house as his wife. He wanted to kiss her.

Ethel looked up. "Everything all right, Jenky? There's not been a turn for the worse?"

Jenky shook his head slowly. "Not yet."

"What do you mean?"

"Nothing. I'd better get these groceries put away at her house. Thank you so much, Ethel." He reached in his wallet and took out a couple of twenties. "This is for what I owe you and the rest is credit for Vi. And here's one more for King's account. He's done some work for me."

Ethel helped him load the purchases into the truck. "Jenky," she said as he got behind the wheel, "you are a good man."

"We shall see," he muttered.

Chapter 7

The Constituency

Reggie rolled along the Hendricks' lane in his Roadster with the top down. The red wheels barely turned. Two strange men were loading a heavy-duty truck with all kinds of machines, tools, and a small concrete mixer. He pulled up to the house and went inside after knocking a few times.

He called out for Violet, but all was quiet. The windows were open and her car was there. Where was she? Probably chopping weeds.

Reg went outside and approached the two men. He smiled and tipped his hat. "Afternoon, gentlemen. I rent a room here. Can you tell me what's going on?"

The older man wiped sweat off his forehead with the back of his arm.

The younger man came up to admire the Roadster. "The lady of the house is in the Cortez hospital. Got poisoned by the storm runoff in her drinking water, most likely from that hog farm on the hill. Now she's got a new well, thanks to her boyfriend, Jenky Butler. Gee, some car you got there."

"Poisoned?" Reg considered his own fate. "How soon did she get sick?"

The older man walked up. "The mailman found her about six days ago, but she's coming home today. Jenky's gonna pick her up when he gets back from the ice house. She sure ought to marry him now. C'mon, son, let's get this rig out of here."

Reg didn't care for the idea of Jenky snatching Violet out of his grasp. He needed a little more time. He got in the Roadster and drove back onto the county road. The red wheels were spinning madly from then on.

~

Jenky grieved over his dilemma. He talked out loud the whole way to Violet's. "The voice of the people must be heard. A representative must choose the many over the few, for the greater good of everyone, not my own personal good. Keep your eye on the goal. Violet will understand. Violet will understand. Violet will *never* understand. Duty calls me. Maybe she should…could…would stay one more night in the hospital. It would be wise for her health. She will come home and try to drive the tractor or hoe weeds. Another night would give her more strength. Now to persuade her of that.

Jenky rounded a curve, hugging the inside, as another car barreled down the middle of the road. It was a narrow miss and the driver was Regal Reg. So he was back. At least he was headed away from Violet's house. Jenky drove down her short lane as the well drillers were packing their equipment to leave. Jenky nodded and raised his hand. The truck driver did likewise.

He took a moment to check the new pump she would use. The cement was still wet around the base. He had an idea as he set the first box of groceries inside on the kitchen table. Bean met him at the door and Jenky carried the purring cat outside to the wet cement. He pressed his front right paw into the soft, cool mixture and then, using his pocket knife, very precisely wrote **BEAN ~ 1939** under the paw print. He used his handkerchief to clean the cat's paw.

~

With all the groceries put away and ice in the box, Jenky filled the vases with water from his bucket and stuck the flowers in. Too bad the roses weren't blooming. They were budding though. If Violet wanted to arrange these substitutes, it would at least keep her in the house. He left one vase on the kitchen table, one on the coffee table in the parlor, and the third on her bedside table next to her kerosene lamp. The new white towel was hung on the door hook and the old one he laid on a shelf in the screened-in porch. He removed the old bedding and replaced it with the crisp sheet set. Last of all, he took out his love letter to her, kissed it and placed it on the pillow closest to the lamp.

The house smelled better. He couldn't wait to bring her inside. All was perfect. Except for the fact that he was supposed to pick her up from the hospital but instead he was headed to Durango to participate in a last-minute conference alongside the Governor. Violet might understand. After all, if she didn't want to spend another night, he could pick her up on his way home later in the evening. Things could still be perfect, especially if she didn't kill him.

~

Violet stood at the window hoping the bird might return. At least she was wearing her own clothes. Annie had washed them for her. They were still stiff from the clothesline. Her last memory of the day when she got sick was of pinning a list of chores to the kitchen curtain.

"Would you like to sit outside to eat?" Annie said, coming in with lunch. "The doctor's wife and her bridge club have fixed up a wonderful patio for patients. There are tables with umbrellas like you see in magazines."

"Sure." Violet put on slippers that someone had brought. "I would really like that."

Annie led the way down the hall to the patio exit. "Nobody knows the value of fresh air to recuperation, that's what I say." She pushed open the door and held it for Violet.

Violet shaded her eyes from the sun. The patio was surrounded with tubs of young petunias and the umbrellas were decorated with blue and white stripes. She sat at one of the tables and ate her ham and cheese sandwich, potato salad, and then drank a tall glass of milk with a slice of cinnamon apple cake. It was a feast.

Afterwards, she rested her elbows on the table and watched a boy and girl sitting under a shady tree in the park across the street. Jenky owed her a kiss. He was about to do it, too, when the doctor interrupted the other day. If he ever did get back around to kissing her, she would make it one he would never forget. She wasn't sure how, but she would figure that out at the time. He should be coming any time now to take her home. If it hadn't been for her encouragement the kiss might never have come. By some miracle, the big rain had somehow brought out Jenky's hidden love.

~

Annie came for her dirty dishes and to give her a pill. "Sunshine is good for you. Now you have color in your cheeks."

"Thank you." Violet downed the pill and sat back in the chair with her eyes closed. She considered whether to give him a little kiss on the cheek when he came for her or keep it to a hug. No need to scare him off.

She heard Annie talking with someone inside and turned to see if it might be Jenky. The patio door opened and Reg walked into the sunshine.

He opened his arms. "I'm gone for a week and you have to be hospitalized. Did you miss me that much, kiddo?" He lifted her out of the chair and kissed her. "You aren't contagious, are you?"

Violet cringed at this unexpected change of characters in her plans. "No. I hope you didn't get sick, too."

Reg sat next to her under the umbrella. He leaned in to kiss her again.

"I hear you are ready to come home. Are you feeling up to snuff?"

"I am kind of back to normal. But not completely normal." Violet could see Annie watching from the patio door. "How did you know I was in the hospital?"

"I get around, kiddo. Hey, what does it take to break you out of here?"

"Jenky is coming to get me. The doctor has to sign me out and tell me to rest. They have all been so wonderful to me."

"Uh-oh. There's a hitch in that plan because I also heard that Jenkins can't make it and I saw him driving towards his house on my way here. Looks like you are stuck with me, beautiful."

Violet frowned at the news of Jenky not coming. Was he sick? She could call Ethel and ask.

Annie stuck her head out the door. "Doctor is here, Violet. You'll need to get back to your room. Alone."

"I have to go," she said and went inside.

"Aces." Reggie smiled. The seed had been planted with plenty of sunshine and sprinkled generously with fertilizer. Now to water it. Romance was no different than raising beans. He pulled his cap over his eyes and propped his feet on the table.

Jenky took the short cut to the hospital. He felt good about his plan to convince Violet to stay another night. It was a ten-bed hospital and four beds were empty, so they had space. He could still get to the meeting with the Governor, spend a few hours, and then pick up Violet before dark if she didn't want to spend another night.

He parked in front and rehearsed a few key lines before going inside.

Nurse Annie was behind the reception desk. "Jenky? I thought you couldn't make it into town today."

He laughed. "Here I am. Is it all right if I go back to see her?"

"Goodness me, sir. Violet left about a half hour ago. She was upset that you couldn't come, though."

He tapped his hat against his leg. "What made Vi think that I wasn't coming?"

Annie held up her hands. "I don't know. She told Dr. Warren and me that she would have to ride with that other fellow because you couldn't make it."

Jenky's jaw snapped open. "Was this other fellow tall with blonde hair and an Eastern accent? Did Vi call him Reg?"

Annie stood. She could see this was a thorny situation. "That's him. Violet called him Reg. He was a kissing fool, too."

Now his jaw was twitching, but he spoke through a politician's smile as he shook her hand. "Thank you, Annie. You have certainly been kind to Violet and have taken such good care of her. Tell Doc Warren that I will see to Vi's bill immediately when all of the charges are final." He put his hat on and was out the door before Annie had time to regret telling him about the kisses.

~

Reg talked the whole way from Cortez to Dove Creek. Violet enjoyed his stories but now she was concerned about Jenky.

"Let's stop at Sitton's so I can talk to Ethel. She'll know if Jenky is ill."

"You don't need to use your energy for that. I'll find out for you later." Reg drove past the store. "He's a big boy and can take care of himself. I think you have lost weight."

Violet had been surveying the farms all the way from Cortez. "Yeah. I probably did." The fields didn't look too bad.

"We'll have to get you back to your hot mama self," Reg said and touched her cheek.

Violet's head swiveled in his direction. "What? Keep your observations to yourself and you're starting to use that 'we' business again."

"You're right. I haven't been around a proper lady like you in a week and I should watch my slap-happy mouth."

"If you lose your manners in a week, then you didn't have many to begin with," Violet said, with her attention still on the bean fields as they turned off the state road and onto her county road.

"When did you get home, anyway?"

Reg shrugged. "Noon today." I met the well drillers, checked their work, and gave them the okay to leave."

"Really. Did you and Jenky work that out or did you take that upon yourself?"

"Why so snippy, kiddo? It's a beautiful day and you are nearly home. It's all aces."

Violet craned her neck to see her fields that were coming into view. "Stop up here, please."

Reg eased to a stop and Violet got out. She folded her arms and stood like that for a bit, surveying her farmland. She inhaled deeply before getting back inside. They turned into her lane.

"I should check the mail." She opened her door and went to the mailbox. It was empty. Tyrel was probably holding it until she came home. Before she went back to the car, Violet saw that new posts had been installed on both sides of her turn-in. She bent down until she could see inside the culvert, even though it made her lightheaded. Jenky probably had one of the Stanley brothers clean it out. That was so kind of him and them. It was a thankless job.

"Now can we go?" Reg asked from the car.

She climbed in and the car rolled the short distance to her house. Reg took his bags and photography equipment to the tack room and Violet went to see her new well pump. She tested it for a few seconds into a bucket and the water appeared with much better pressure than she'd ever had before. The concrete wasn't set yet around the pump. That's when she noticed the paw print and the printing. Only Jenky could print so perfectly. She smiled. Surely he wasn't sick from the water. She could drive over the hill and check on him. But first, she wanted to see Bean. He was waiting inside and she gave him all the petting he could stand. This was the longest she had ever been away from her house. It was familiar but also somehow strange to her. She was about to take a stroll around when Reg came in.

"Anything I can do for you, kiddo?" he asked. "I don't suppose there's anything to eat in here." He opened the ice box. "I supposed wrong. This thing is loaded." He opened the pantry. "Bingo again."

Violet followed his tour of things. "Gosh. I've never had this much food in the ice box or the pantry."

"Well, looky here," Reg said, opening a box of chocolates. "My favorite kind, too."

"And flowers," Violet said as she caressed the petals with her fingertips. She recognized the deep pink tulips and bright daffodils. Mrs. Butler always shared them with her mother. The vases all belonged to Jenky's mother. Where was he?

Reg helped himself to another chocolate and moved to the parlor and beyond.

"More flowers," Violet said when she discovered the vase in the parlor. She turned towards her bedroom as Reg emerged.

"What were you doing in my bedroom?"

He winked at her. "Looking for more chocolate."

Violet saw the blossoms on her bedside table. She noticed also the new pillowcases on her bed. They were perfect, with a blue ribbon trim.

She raised the covers and checked. It was a completely new set of bed linens. She would sleep in heavenly comfort tonight, even if she were still alone.

The screen door smacked shut which meant Reg had left. Hopefully, there was one piece of chocolate left in the box for her.

～

Reg held the envelope he'd found on her pillow. To my sweet Violet it read. The writing was meticulous, like an old maid schoolmarm's. He ran his finger under the flap and drew out the letter. The paper was unlined and high quality. As though this politician would use any other kind. He lay on his bed and read the letter twice before sticking it back in the envelope. He exhaled and pursed his lips. The old boy was first-rate in his writing skills, but he probably couldn't deliver in person. That's why this most delicious woman was still single and available for his purposes.

Reg's lips curved into a crooked smile. He could lift the passionate prose from the politician's letter but put it into his own words, like piggy-backing off a Hollywood script. The thought heightened his senses and made him hungry and thirsty. He reached into his knapsack and pulled out a bottle of whiskey. Oh, he did relish a romantic challenge, especially one that involved worthy competition.

～

The dim light from kerosene lamps in Violet's house let Jenky know that she was home. He also saw a glow in the tack room where Ruthless *Reg* must be plotting his next wicked scheme to steal Violet's heart. Of course Violet might be eager to go along with any such scheme with Reg, but she was in favor of a kiss in the hospital. Jenky drove by at such a slow speed, his car died and he had to restart it. It occurred to him that his car dying was a sign from above that he should turn down the lane, confront Reg, and explain things to Vi.

She would have read his letter by now and knew beyond any doubt where he stood in their relationship. A love letter wasn't the best way to go. He should have told her in the hospital. He told himself that if Reg weren't there, he would have stopped. At this point, he wasn't sure but what he might take a swing at Reg for whisking Violet out of the hospital under false pretenses. Perhaps in the larger picture they weren't false pretenses, but Jenky was the only person who knew that he had to go to Durango today. Reg had fabricated a story that was only half true.

Jenky had, after all, gone by the hospital to discuss the situation with her. He drove over the hill to his home and sat in the truck. Caesar sat next to it and waited for his wishy-washy master to get out. Which he did, eventually.

～

Vi turned out her lamp and savored the luxury of her new sheets. The colorful blooms next to the bed added to her moment of bliss. Only if she knew what happened to Jenky, would she have been more serene. No. If Jenky were lying beside her, that would top everything. It could be that he had to go back to Denver for some reason, but surely he would have told her about it in person. And what was Reg doing in the tack room? Even after supper had been brought to the door by Bessie Stanley, he still didn't show up.

Tomorrow she would go to Sitton's and talk with Ethel about Jenky's sudden departure and then her energy would be directed into her bean crop. Something, though, was not right as to Jenky's whereabouts. She sent up a fervent prayer that he was all right before she closed her weary eyes. In the not too distant hills, a gang of coyotes yipped into the summer night.

～

Reg showed up for breakfast as Violet was leaving. He looked pathetic and smelled worse. "There are biscuits, gravy, and ham in the cupboard," she told him. "You do recall that I have a no-alcohol rule."

He scowled at her. "Don't talk so loud."

"A friend of mine is coming by to milk the cow and take care of the chickens." She shut the screen door, then reopened it. "Who told you that Jenky couldn't pick me up yesterday?"

"I don't remember," Reg mumbled.

Violet got in the Maxwell and stewed. It very well could be that Reg had a drinking problem. She would address that issue later. Now she had to find out about Jenky. At the top of her lane, rather than turning right, towards Dove Creek, she turned left, towards Jenky's.

～

The lane to the Butler's beautiful house always reminded Violet of a fairy tale book illustration where the road didn't go straight, but curved in an S shape to a gradual rise which overlooked a portion of their front acreage. That's where they'd built their home. Jenky's mother was an accomplished gardener, and he had kept things up in her memory, so things hadn't changed much over the years.

Caesar ran to greet her and she leaned down to hug him. Jenky came out to the porch.

She smiled sweetly. "Hi. I was worried that you had gotten sick from your water, too. What happened yesterday?"

Jenky couldn't quite look her way. "I came to the hospital but you had already left."

Violet rose up. "What? Reg said that you weren't coming at all." She opened the wrought iron gate and went up the stone pathway to him. They embraced but there was no kissing. "Let's sit on the chairs. I'm still a little lightheaded." She took his hand.

His nervousness was noticeable. "Sure. I should have suggested that right away. Other than lightheadedness, are you better?"

"I'm not sure how I'm supposed to feel, but it's better than down and out."

Jenky drummed his fingers on the chair arm. "I came by the hospital to see if you would consider spending one more night or if I could pick you up about seven o'clock." His story came to an unexpected halt.

Violet prodded. "Because…"

"I got a call from Governor Carr yesterday at noon. He was in Durango for a conference that included the status of REA's progress for our district. It's coming, Vi. This time next year, your house will be wired."

She unclasped his hand and stared at the concrete porch. "Did you go to Durango?"

He took that as a bad sign. "Well, naturally, the Governor wanted me there for the REA portion of the conference." Violet's head jerked towards him, then away. "I had to go, Vi. I needed to see the direction to take my support. I don't know when or where your tenant got the idea that I couldn't come at all. I assume he made it up. Did you read my letter?"

Violet stood, her hands in tight fists. "You thought that I could wait at the hospital, even stay another night, so that you could glad-hand and kiss the Governor's boots?"

Jenky stood next to her. "I'm not a glad-hander or boot-kisser, Vi. You know that. I wanted to be the one to bring you home and carry you into your house. I had planned everything so perfectly, then he called and I had to put the interests of my constituents over my personal agenda in this situation. You can appreciate that." His hands were out like a juggler with a dozen bowling pins in the air.

She faced him with a fierceness he'd never seen before. "Jenky Butler, you know what I think? You can snuggle up to your precious constituents for the rest of your days for all I care. It wasn't a choice of *them* over your *personal agenda*. It was choosing whatever your current interest is over *me*. Just like you have done since we got out of high school. So, there you go. Have a happy life."

Violet left as fast as she could down the steps, but Jenky was right behind. He moved in front of her and held her like a bear hugging a tree. She did not relax against him.

"Did you read my letter?" he asked again, trying desperately to look into her weeping eyes.

She lifted her chin and her words spilled out like a gulley washer. "I don't know what you are talking about and I really don't care. This has gone on long enough, Jenky. It is ridiculous and embarrassing. Let me go."

"This makes no difference, Violet. It doesn't change us." When she refused to answer, he loosened his grip, and she mustered the energy to make swift work of the walk to her car. Caesar went with her, his herding instincts telling him that the master wanted her back in the fold. He nudged her with his body but Violet ignored him. She started the Maxwell and disappeared down the lane.

～

Jenky held his head in his hands and looked with desperation towards the sky and back to the lane. An unfortunate, clay flower pot was between him and the gate. Jenky took two steps and booted it over the fence in an impressive arc. It landed in the lane and shattered like an egg. Caesar went straightaway to investigate, but Jenky went back inside his safe haven house.

～

Violet stopped her car once she was out of sight. She laid her head on the steering wheel and cried. He would never change. His was empty talk at the hospital and she was an idiot to think it might be otherwise. From now on, when Representative Butler entered her mind, she would rip him right out. If he was married to his constituency, then she should look elsewhere for a husband. It was overdue.

Chapter 8
The Kiss

Reginald sat at the kitchen table like he owned the place. He watched her every move. "What can I do to help? I don't know anything about farming, but if it will make your life easier, I can learn." That sounded good. She had been in a snit too long.

"It's weed chopping time." Violet said without humor.

"I can hoe. I might not last very long, but I'll try. Just show me where to go. If I hoe, then you have to let me take more photos of you. Deal? And we need to fatten you up."

"Shouldn't you be taking pictures of people chopping weeds instead of chopping them yourself?" Violet put two fried eggs on his plate already loaded with biscuits and ham. She set the iron skillet on the stove and wiped her hands on her apron. "Why do you want to take my picture? I've never seen the ones you've already taken. As to my weight, I am not a hog to be fattened up, and more than that, it is none of your business."

"Easy, now." He shook salt and pepper on his eggs. "It keeps me on my toes to practice. I can see which lenses are best in this Western light. The altitude makes a difference."

"I don't believe that for one minute." Violet pointed her oatmeal spoon at him. "I did read an article that the hour after the sunrise and the hour before sunset are the best times for photography."

"Where did you read that?"

"In a detective story. They were trying to catch a bad guy who was a photographer."

"Do you think I'm a bad guy?" Reg bumped her knees with his under the table as he grinned.

She looked right at him. "I don't know what to think about you."

"What if I said you take my breath away every time I see you?"

"I wouldn't believe you because you lied about altitude affecting photography." She got him another biscuit. "I can see that altitude would be a concern as to how the atmosphere might affect a photo through excess moisture if you were jumping out of a plane."

Reg stopped chewing. "What are you some kind of brainy broad?"

"Don't call me a broad. I read more than comic books." She changed the topic. "Were you serious about hoeing?"

"Well...I should be taking photos. I assume that if it is weed chopping time, that will be going on all over the county. I'll have to drive around and see, but I do want to help you."

"That makes no sense. You can't hoe from your convertible."

He pushed his chair back and watched her for a minute.

"You do take my breath away when you wear those dresses and makeup. I think about those perfect lips when I'm not with you and if I were to be with you all the time, I'd be kissing them all the time." He didn't wait for her response. He left her with those words.

Violet cleaned the dishes with water she'd brought in earlier from the new pump, but it was Reg's words that were on her mind. Who wouldn't like to hear things like that from a handsome man? He had promised her that he wasn't drinking on her place, but that he only had an upset stomach the other day. He had been so sweet and good to her since she got out of the hospital. She was stronger every day, especially since so many local ladies had brought a big supper every evening. Now she was doing her own chores. The new water trough and feeders in the henhouse did not escape her notice, but she would not dwell on gestures of kindness by the wily representative. He was nothing more to her now than a benevolent neighbor. Mr. Magee, however, was something else—a dreamy distraction.

Jenky would not make another all-night trip to Denver. He loaded his pickup with belongings and books that he normally left at home. He lashed a tarp securely across the load. He hoped that having this stuff would console him at the boarding house in Denver. He must move on with his life.

Vi had never looked at him the way she did on the porch that terrible day. It went straight to his heart and caught there like a bitter pill that wouldn't melt away. If she could react that way towards him after reading his love letter, then she must not care for him as much as he loved her. He would dedicate himself to the people of Colorado and perhaps make Violet proud to say she knew him. If that was the only relationship he could have with her, then so be it. Apparently, he wasn't cut out to be a lover man.

The next morning, Jenky started his trip at precisely five o'clock. He rolled the windows down to wake himself after a mostly sleepless night. Caesar was wide awake and sitting next to him. He topped the hill and saw the small glimmer of a lantern as Violet was probably walking out to milk the cow and feed the chickens. He longed to be with her, laughing and teasing, rather than running off to hide from reality in Denver. The pain from the last few weeks hit him hard at that moment. He wanted to turn down her lane and at least say goodbye, but he had always avoided emotional confrontations. *Go on, do it. Don't be an eternal chicken.* Jenky slowed his truck to a stop and saw the lantern do the same. He turned the steering wheel toward her house with shaking hands.

Violet stood next to the Maxwell with a milk bucket in one hand and a lantern in the other. Her hair was pulled back and she was wearing the shirt and overalls he'd given her. She didn't move. He got out but left his truck running.

"Morning, Vi," he said in a husky voice. He could see that she was breathing fast, so either she was boiling mad or she was curious.

"Morning, Representative. I see you are packed and ready to serve your constituents. Is there something I can help you with?"

"Nope. Just this…" Jenky held her face in both his hands and kissed her with such passion that she dropped the bucket and the lantern. Violet's arms were stuck out like a china doll all through the wild kiss and when it was over, Jenky went back to his truck and left her standing in the red glow of his tail lights. The only chickens around at that moment were snoozing away in the henhouse.

Violet was bamboozled and frozen in time. Was that the Edward Jenkins Butler she had known since her memories began? How many more of those kisses did he have in him? Why did he wait ten years to kiss her like that?

"Gosh, Jenky," she said as his car lights faded down the road. She grabbed her lantern and milk bucket and looked at Bean. "Why did he have to go and do that?"

Bean yawned and trotted ahead of his mistress to the barn since Violet was moving like a snail.

⁓

Violet combed her house, looking for the mysterious letter that Jenky had mentioned twice on the day she told him off. What was he talking about? Was it possible that he had forgotten to give it to her or he dropped it somewhere and didn't notice? He was absent-minded sometimes. She did find her yet unwrapped, second episode edition of Superman. It must have come while she was ill.

Reg knocked on the door. "Where's breakfast? I want to complain to the management." He came right in and kissed her on the forehead. "Seriously, where's the food?"

She blushed. "I got busy. Sit down and I'll get it going. The stove's hot."

"I like to watch you cook. You are like a magic fairy who can wave her wand and the food soon appears." Reg pulled her onto his lap. "Let's work up a little appetite." He kissed her neck and was headed for her lips when she whacked his leg with a wooden spoon. "Hey," he squealed. "What was that for?"

"It was only a tap from my magic wand," she said with a bright smile. "If we start with that kind of stuff, breakfast will be burned."

"Oh." Reg rubbed his leg. "I'm visiting the Ute Mountain Ute Tribe tomorrow. Have you heard of them?"

"Of course. Haven't you seen the Sleeping Ute Mountain near Cortez?"

"Nah. But I suppose I will now. I may have to do more talking than photography this first trip. I should get a room at a motor inn for the night if Cortez has one. It's slow going on the road from here to there. The state needs to pave it. Thanks," he said as Violet tipped the frying pan full of scrambled eggs into his plate.

She poured water from the kettle into the frying pan to soak the egg fragments, and then sat across from him as she added milk to her oatmeal. "There's one in Cortez and it would save you driving time and using gas. Are you finished with your farm assignment? You have been taking lots of tribal pictures lately."

"I sent the last of my rolls of film to my boss. They are very interested in regional tribes and want me to pursue that, too. Someone else will write the article…not me. I can't write anything very well."

"You are good with words around me," Violet said then sipped her coffee.

He narrowed his eyes. "I'd like to put those words into action, landlady. How about we take some pictures this morning?"

She rinsed out her coffee cup and set it on the windowsill. "You've already lost the golden hour, plus one of us has work to do. Could you please put your scraps in the bucket and set your plate in that dishpan on the left?"

"Will do. Where are you going and what am I supposed to do while you're gone?"

"I'm your landlady, not your nanny. I have to work on my tractor."

"Could I watch? Might be some great photo shots."

Violet laughed. "Yeah, sure. Me lying on my back with engine oil in my eye."

He knelt before her. "Come on—please."

How could she turn him down when he was on one knee and kissing her hand?

~

"I am not wearing a dress to change the oil on my tractor," Violet said, giggling at the thought.

Reg dug around in the trunk of his Roadster. "Then how about this blouse? You could wear it with your overalls. Aces. Problem solved—something for you and something for me. Pin this silk flower in your hair, too."

She held up the red blouse. "It looks like a flamenco dancer's with all the ruffles and elastic."

Reg closed the trunk. "You'll have on your overalls anyway."

"Oh, please," she said as she took the blouse to her room. She came right back out with it on and the flower in her hair. "This is silly. I sure hope nobody sees me wearing a flower in my hair, a flamenco blouse, and overalls while I change the oil."

"Where I come from, the fellows would line up for blocks to see you in that blouse."

She pulled up on the bib of her overalls. "Dove Creek is not where you come from, though."

~

He followed Violet to her tool shed. She came out with a variety of tools and went to the Farmall. She lay right on the ground, slid the pan under the tractor, and unscrewed something causing dirty brown liquid to spew out and into the pan while Reg moved around snapping the whole thing with his camera. Violet shook her head at him while she wiped her hands on a rag. She loosened another bolt, lifted something from a spindle, and exchanged it with a newer-looking part. It was all a magic trick to Reg, but she sure looked like a million bucks while she did it.

She started the engine and watched the needle on a gauge.

"You are the kind of woman that men write songs about, Violet," Reg said, above the putt-putt of the tractor engine.

She put her hand to her ear. "What? I can't hear you."

Reg shouted. "You are the kind of woman that men…"

Violet turned off the engine. "That men…what?"

He moved very near and nuzzled his lips close to her ear. "That drives men crazy," Reg said and kissed her while still holding his camera.

～

She had become used to having Reggie around, but although he was gone overnight at various times, Violet didn't truly miss him. She missed talking to someone besides Bean, but she didn't mind the fact that she could eat when and what she wanted and that there weren't as many dishes to wash or as much water to haul.

The last time she heated water for him to bathe, he fell asleep and didn't use it at all. He was fun to be around and very flattering, but Violet figured that he had been around the block too many times from the way he looked at her and tried little tricks to get her to do things she wouldn't. But no man on earth could ever match Jenky's kiss the morning he left. Nobody.

～

Caesar had brought his leash to Jenky three times without any acknowledgement that, yes, he would take him for a walk. The fourth time, Caesar proffered his paw on Jenky's knee. His master gave him a good scratching behind his ears. Caesar whined.

"Oh, is it time to go outside?" Jenky asked, finally. "Sorry, boy. I was thinking about something else."

Caesar ran to the door and back. Jenky put on his fedora and attached the leash to Caesar's collar. "Let's go."

They walked down to St. John's Cathedral, their usual route, but on the way back, Jenky took a different route in order to pass by the tavern where he'd seen the beer poster. It was still in the window and he examined it closely. Soon, the barkeep appeared in the doorway.

"May I help you, sir?" the stodgy man asked.

Jenky pointed at the poster. "Where do you get these?"

The man joined him on the sidewalk. "She's a beauty, huh? They come from a calendar company in California about six times a year. I figure the brewer hires them to come up with poster ads. Why?"

Jenky blushed. "The lady looks exactly like an old friend of mine, that's all. I'm curious how she got into the modeling business. I can't see the artist's name. It's blocked by the window frame."

"I'll see if there's a business name on the back. You got a minute?"

"Sure. That would be swell." Jenky watched as the man lifted the poster and examined the front and back. His throat tightened.

The fellow returned quickly. "The artist signature is Vorhees and the stamp on the back is *Pacific Coast Calendar Company, Los Angeles, California*."

"Thank you, sir." Jenky looked at the poster in the window one more time. Violet would never have her picture taken with her shoulder bare and showing so much bosom. Then he went back to the doorway. The man inside was behind the bar now. "I'd like to have that poster when you get a new one. I'll pay you for it. My name is Edward." It was the truth. "My phone number is on the card."

The fellow nodded and slipped the card into the cash register. "No charge. I'll give you a call."

He felt good, acting on his obsession with the poster. They walked briskly to the nearest park and Jenky took off Caesar's leash and let him run around before going back to the office. Now he could concentrate and move on with state business.

∽

As soon as he filled Caesar's water bowl and gave him a dog biscuit, Jenky called the Los Angeles operator for the phone number of the Pacific Coast Calendar Company. He wrote it in big letters and numbers, circled it and propped the paper next to Violet's high school senior picture. This poster business smacked of Reginald Magee, he felt it in his gut. The phone number nagged at him, too, as he worked on the wording of a bill proposal. He finally picked up the phone again and called the company. He was directed to an overly friendly man with a tinny voice in the sales department.

"I am thinking about having my business name on one of your calendars. Exactly how does that work?" Jenky asked.

"Terrific. That's terrific. We make it easy for that to happen for our clients. You've come to the right place. We have the fastest turnaround in the business. From the time you sign a contract with us to the time you are handing out calendars to your customers, it will be less than a month. Our art department can supply you with a catalog of choices or you can customize your calendar art. We have everything from travel scenes to pinup girls."

Jenky raised an eyebrow. "I saw a poster for McDoull's Beer that I really liked. The artist signed it 'Vorhees'. Could I get the same artist to make a calendar for me?"

"Going for the pinups, eh? I don't blame you. Vorhees is excellent and fast. He can use live models or submitted photographs. I've seen him take a fully clothed model and draw her with nothing on but her birthday suit in one day." The man snickered. "His work catches every man's eye, *gare-on-teed.*"

"Pardon?"

"Business joke. Means *guaranteed.*"

Jenky did not find that information humorous at all. He considered it most disturbing. "You have been very helpful. Can I call you back when I decide for sure?"

"Yes, sir." He gave Jenky his direct phone number.

Jenky leaned back in his chair. He had nothing yet to prove what he was thinking. And Vi would be furious should this theory of his turn out to be wrong and he had foolishly confided it to her. If he went any further, he had to have the proper justification. It shouldn't be to crush Reginald, like the cow pie that he was, it would have to be pursued solely in order to protect the honor and integrity of sweet Violet. But it sure would be fun to see Reggie Magee on the trot from Dove Creek to save his sorry hide. What a deceiving, unworthy, malicious man.

Jenky slammed his fists down on the arms of his chair. "You son of a gun!" Caesar's ears perked up. "Not you, boy."

Violet draped her holey old towel over the window of the back door for privacy, and closed the kitchen curtains, not that anybody else was around, just for her own modesty. The water was boiling on the stove already. She carefully poured it into the tub as the bar of homemade soap in the bottom bubbled into foam. That made her happy because she had added a little castor oil to her most recent soap batch so it would make a foamy lather for her bath. The second pan of water began to boil. She poured it in, then added a bucket of cold water. She undressed and stepped into the wonderful water. After a day of chopping weeds in the field, the only thing better would be a bigger tub…a bigger *porcelain* tub with warm water coming right from the tap. And she would need soap that smelled like lilacs or honeysuckle. Jenky had already bought her a fluffy towel. Oh, that kiss. Gosh.

While she soaked, two more pans were warming up to wash her hair. It was an exciting day because she now had a store-bought bottle of shampoo, thanks to the credit balance Jenky had set up at Sitton's. No more mixing up her mother's recipe for hair washing soap. When the steam began rising off the pans, Violet reached for her towel and stepped out of the tub and onto an old dishtowel. She moved the pans to the kitchen table and washed her hair in one and rinsed it in the other. She took her old towel off the door and wrapped it around her head and began drying herself with her fluffy new one. A tiny flash of light caught her eye—maybe another thunderstorm was coming. She turned again when she heard a rustling sound. Bean meowed. Violet covered herself with the towel and peeked out the window. She hoped it wasn't a skunk after her chickens. Reggie would be back soon, though, so she'd better hurry and get dressed to cook supper.

⌇

Later, rather than smelling like something much worse, Reg came in the kitchen with the heavy, pungent fragrance of sagebrush on his clothing. Bean went to the parlor, sneezing all the way.

"You must have had a busy day," Violet said as she filled his plate with fried chicken, pinto beans, biscuits and gravy. "I like that smell. At least for five minutes."

"This looks good, kiddo. Yeah, lots of sagebrush and something called rabbitbrush. Interesting country and people. I got some ace photos." Reg talked between gulps of food.

"Did you like the motor inn?" Obviously, the man was starving.

"It was okay, but…" He closed his eyes. "My time away from you is painful. Every new scene is framed with images of you. All my thoughts are jam-packed with 'what would Violet think about this'. In other words, kiddo, you and I are together, even when we are apart, at least for me."

Violet stopped eating with a bite in midair. "That's beautiful, Reg. I don't know what to think. What…are you saying about us?"

"I'm saying what you are hearing, Vi. I am serious." He reached for another biscuit.

Violet laid her fork on her plate. "Is this about love between you and me?"

"Well…yeah…if you put it that way. Sure."

She studied him. "Now isn't the right time to talk about this."

He looked up from his food. "Tell me how you feel about me."

"I…like you. You make me laugh, but I'm not sure I love you."

"Really?" Reg drew back. "But that's not to say you won't or can't love me. We need to keep things going. Give love a chance to breathe."

People in Hollywood and New York might talk that way, but not here in Dove Creek.

Violet sighed. "Just exactly how do you give love a chance to *breathe*, Reg?"

He closed his eyes again, leaned back in his chair, and recited:

> *Love is a smoke made without lies,*
> *It comes from the fire I see in your eyes,*
> *I am lost in an old sea of past fears.*
> *But I will never bring you sadness or tears.*
> *What else can it be? It is love, my sweet,*
> *I now place my heart and soul at your feet.*

Violet listened, but with downcast eyes. "Gosh, Reg. You are a man of surprises. Who wrote that?"

He paused as though he was trying to remember. "I forgot. But it says a lot."

She was lost to him for a moment.

He scraped his plate clean. "This supper was aces. Now, is there anything sweet? Other than you, of course."

Violet stirred. "Umm…not tonight. I'll make shortcake tomorrow if I have time. There's jam in the pantry to put on top."

Reg leaned across the table for a kiss. "Can you whip up some cream, too?"

"You could help me. It might be a way to let things breathe."

"I could take photos of you while you cook. Put on that cute little apron of yours. What do you say?" He beamed, full of mischief.

"You can't take any more pictures of me until I see the old ones. That's that." Violet began clearing the table. "What are you doing with them anyway—making a scrapbook?"

He took the dirty dishes out of her hands and kissed her. How about we go to the porch and I'll recite that poem again. I know you liked it."

She smiled. "I did. It might sound even better when you don't have a mouthful of food."

"You're so picky." Reg twirled her around and began singing, "It don't mean a thing if it ain't got that swing…" He danced a giggling Violet through the parlor and onto the front porch.

~

King moved his fence back about twenty feet from the embankment overlooking Violet's farm. He set the posts in deep and shored them up tight. He strung new barbed wire thanks to the credit Jenky had given him at Sitton's. Now he stood on the crest of the embankment watching Violet wield a hoe. That young lady worked all day, every day, except for Sunday mornings. He had seen her from his corner at church. She always sat in the back, alone.

He was turning away when he noticed her scaredy-cat renter walking towards where Violet was working. He sure didn't have a hoe with him. In fact, he must have a camera in his hand because he began taking pictures of her right away. At least that's what it seemed to King that he was doing. Then the renter started kissing her more than he was taking photos. That's when King decided to stop looking. He picked up his tools and went to his house, spitting a couple of times. That renter was up to no good. He had something going on and kept Violet on the hook with his romancing nonsense. Jenky was too good of a man to lose Violet to a nogoodnik. That one needed to take a running leap off a tall cliff.

~

"National Geographic Society. How may I help you?" The lady who answered his call had no idea how nervous Jenky was.

"This is Representative Butler from Colorado and I'm trying to contact someone who is a photographer for you."

"Is he on staff or a contracted photographer?" she asked.

"I'm not sure."

"I will transfer you to the photography department. One moment, please."

Jenky told the same story again and again. Then he hit pay dirt with a supervisor.

"Sure. Reggie works for us. He's on assignment now in the West.

Should I have him call you?"

Jenky grimaced. "No, no, no. I only needed verification of his affiliation. Thank you very much." He hung up before any more questions could be raised. So, Reggie was who he said he was, but apparently, he was also slightly more than that. Jenky might as well go ahead and order his calendar.

He dialed the number for the Pacific Coast Calendars and the annoying salesperson answered.

Jenky cleared his throat. "I have decided to place an order for a calendar."

"Good for you. You are the pinup man, right?"

He turned red. "I'm not sure I would put it that way, but I do have a request."

"Absolutely. You name it. We are out to please. Let me get the vital information first. Your name?"

"Edward Caesar," Jenky said, patting Caesar's head as he fabricated his story.

"Name, address, and the nature of your business," the salesman asked.

"Caesar's Luxury Bath Fixtures. That should speak for itself." Jenky gave a newly rented post office box number for delivery and the physical address of a vacant lot in Denver to be printed on the calendar.

The salesman laughed. "You've been flushing business down the toilet. Get the joke? All that will change once you start passing around our calendars."

"Yes, hopefully." Jenky chewed on his lip.

"Okay, then. The calendars are sold in units of a dozen, with a five dozen minimum."

Sixty calendars to *burn*. "Five dozen is fine, but my stipulation is that I only want all the existing illustrations of the model we discussed the other day for my calendar."

"You're talking about Vorhees' pastel of the good looker lying in the buttercups with her dress slipping down her arm and showing plenty of what she's got?"

Jenky reddened up again. "Yes. Use that one and any others that he's done of the same model. Ask him how much he would charge for the original?"

"No sir. I can't do that. Vorhees works for Pacific Coast Calendar and all artwork officially belongs to them. Your order will be filled and shipped within the next ten business days, as soon as you get a check to us for $17.58, that is. That includes shipping charges, of course."

"Of course." He wrote the figure in his notebook. "Thank you. I am expecting a quality product."

"We don't make anything else."

The call was over, but Jenky had a guilty conscience over his fictitious business. He changed his mind when the phone rang.

"Is this Edward?" The caller asked.

Was the salesman checking on his business? No. He hadn't used his office number.

"Yes, this is Edward."

"I have that poster for you. We got a new one today. You may want it, too, when you see it."

~

Jenky and Caesar were at the tavern in fifteen minutes. He picked up the old one and thanked the barkeep. The new poster was in the window and it made Jenky want to punch Risqué Reg Magee's smart aleck look right off his face. The woman was unmistakably Violet standing in front of her honeysuckle vine. She was holding Bean against her cheek and wearing a fancy dress. The caption was Make your honey purr like a kitten. Buy her a McDoull's. Vi's neckline, however, revealed more bosom outside the dress than was hidden inside the dress. Jenky would indeed make the lowly snake pay the very next time he saw him. Violet had to be told somehow. The problem was she would never believe it about Reg unless she saw the illustrations with her own eyes. Jenky didn't want to be around when that happened, or maybe he did.

~

He had actually gotten some work done at the office the last few days. It was quiet there when the assembly was not in session. As he was entertaining that thought, the phone rang.

"Governor Carr for you, Jenky," the secretary said.

"All right. I'm listening."

The Governor didn't hesitate. "Jenky, you need to get down to Montezuma County as well as Dolores County area, spread the word and stir up support for the REA. They'll be going door to door once the paperwork is done and the loan money is signed for. They've had all kinds of roadblocks with this. Rights of way, liability insurance policies, and hiring qualified power line workers. Can you arrange to go home say, week after next? The Board down there has lost a lot of sleep to get this thing off to a running start, but folks have to know what to expect and how they go about joining and getting their houses wired. The Board has done a real bang up job. Now we need to boost the effort to get the word out…and *Power On, Colorado*…that's the word. Jenky, are you there?"

"Yes, sir. I am waiting my turn to speak."

"Well, here's your chance. Can you go?"

"With pleasure. I'll get out a letter to the Board right now."

"That's the spirit. Generations to come will thank you. Goodbye now."

That's the way conversations seemed to go with the passionate governor. Jenky placed the phone back on its hook and checked the dates. The calendars should arrive in plenty of time.

Violet spotted Reg as she drove the tractor in from the nether bean fields. He'd better watch out. Her body ached and her skin was a grimy mixture of dirt and sweat. That's what a day of chopping weeds got her. The Farmall saved her from a tiring walk back to the house. She killed the engine and plopped the can over the exhaust.

"Hello, gorgeous," Reg said, lighting a cigarette. "What's for supper?"

Violet shot him a piercing look. "Bathwater," she said, heading for the house.

"No, I'm serious. I got another paycheck today and I thought we could go to Dove Creek and buy a fountain drink. Does anybody cook hamburgers this side of Cortez?"

Violet stopped. "You are going to buy me a meal?"

He turned his head to avoid blowing smoke on her. "Sure. I'm a generous guy. Then we can come back and snuggle on the front porch."

Bean rubbed against her leg. "I have to take a bath first. It was blistering hot out there today."

"Can you hurry? I'm hungry and it's Saturday night. They actually show movies in Dove Creek sometimes on Saturday nights. I bet you didn't know that."

Violet reached inside the screened-in porch and handed Reg two buckets. "This will help hurry my bath time. Fill both of those at the pump. I'll build a fire in the stove and put the pans on top. You can pour the water into the pans, right?"

"Could be. Will there be snuggling on the porch later?"

"Just fill the dang buckets. Honestly, Reg."

"Okay, okay. Don't get so worked up. It only seems logical to me that if you are so hot, you'd like a cooler bath, that's all."

Violet went in the house, but not quietly. "If I wanted a cool bath, I would have jumped into the creek," she shouted from the kitchen.

Reg smiled. Not a bad idea for a photo session.

～

"How did you spend your time today?" Violet asked, as the breezy ride in the convertible cooled her temper.

"I made extra notes for my photo files of the trip to Utah. I do that to help the writers."

She turned to him. "Ah, you have the photos back from your trip to Utah. That means you must also have the pictures of me. You took those earlier and I want to see them."

He threw out his cigarette. "I can arrange that. They turned out aces."

Violet looked him over. He really was an attractive man—sort of college boy dashing. Just keep him away from pigs. She grinned at the memory of him running out of the privy when King's big hog was snuffling around it. And who could forget the sight of that same boar chasing him uphill from the creek the day that Jenky saw... She let that recollection go for the time being. It was too painful.

⌒

The crickets were ear-splitting loud. "Do you think it's a plague?" Reg asked.

Violet yawned. "I hope not. My beans don't need that."

"I know what you need." Reg kissed her and tried to sneak his hands where she didn't want them to go.

"That's it. I am going to bed," Violet said and got to her feet from the porch steps.

He stood, too. "Want some company? I get lonesome in the tack room. It makes me think I'm always in the doghouse."

"You could get in the doghouse really fast if you don't keep your hands to yourself." He probably rolled his eyes at her, but she couldn't tell in the dark.

"Wait." He rubbed his forehead. "Am I supposed to kiss you with my hands behind my back? You know, in my heart, I long to touch your skin and to commit it to memory so that I can always recall the memory in my fingers."

Violet's nose wrinkled. "What are you talking about? That makes no sense. In fact, you've been doing that a lot lately."

"Hold on." Reg sat on the steps again and whispered to himself before responding. "I long to memorize the sensation of my precious skin touching yours in my heart. Wait, wait...I know that an intense passion, a deep longing, survives between us. I have always felt it when we touch. I carry that memory in my heart, as I wait to touch you again." He grinned. "There you go—aces. Woohoo on you, Magee!"

Violet sat on the steps beside him. "You say that you can't write. I beg to differ, Reg. Your words stay in my heart, even if they are odd."

"Then let's try that kiss again," he said, and they did.

~

The thin notice of "a package too large to fit" fluttered slightly as he opened his post office box. Jenky took the notice straight to a service window and handed it to a middle-aged man wearing a red, white, and blue visor. The man returned with a medium-sized box.

"Got far to go?" the man asked. "This is on the heavy side."

"Thanks. I'm a farm boy at heart. It couldn't be worse than a bale of hay." Jenky hefted the box to his left shoulder, took Caesar's leash in his right hand, and was out the door. The box was heavy. Sixty large calendars. What could he do with them except burn them all but one. That one Vi had to see.

Rather than leave them at his apartment or office, Jenky took them to his truck. He rolled the windows down and, with his pocket knife, carefully opened the box. Each set of a dozen was wrapped in thin butcher paper. Before ripping into a set, Jenky took a deep breath and told himself that only the workers in the Pacific Coast Calendar Company had seen these affronts to Violet's modesty and privacy.

He slid the top one out and flipped through the *1940 calendar compliments of Caesar's Deluxe Bath Fixtures*. There she was, his lovely, sweet, and innocent Violet gracing each month with her beautiful smile but in various stages of immodest dress or partial undress until December. The December illustration made him sick. Violet was looking right at the camera, lips puckered, wearing nothing but a Santa hat. A washtub full of bubbles was next to her. Jenky ground his teeth and chucked the calendar into the floorboard.

Jenky sensed the flush of fury on his face. He started the engine and drove off so fast that Caesar lost his footing on the seat and quickly lay down with his head resting on the culprit box of calendars.

~

Violet's hand basket was full. She sat it on the counter so Ethel could ring it up.

"We have dresses on sale right now, dear. Would you like to see them?"

Violet took her coin purse out of the bib pocket of her overalls. "Nice try, Ethel. Some day when I'm rich, I'll walk in here and buy every dress you have."

Ethel placed her purchases in a small box. "That will be a dollar and eleven cents. Jenky will be in town this weekend."

Goosebumps spread over her. "What's the occasion?"

"Howard got a letter, he's on the REA board you know, saying that Jenky is coming to show state support for the big REA push next spring. He's speaking at the high school gym in Cortez at two o'clock and at our dance at the Grange Hall at seven-thirty."

Violet glanced at Ethel. "Thank you."

Ethel watched her leave. She had a feeling that Violet might show up for the dance. It would be preferable if her smart aleck boarder stayed home. There wasn't a soul in Dolores County that didn't know Reggie Magee was standing between Violet and Jenky getting married.

~

"Hey, kiddo, is it okay if I photograph a family in your living room or parlor, whatever you call it?" Reg asked at breakfast the next day.

Violet refilled their coffee cups. "Who and when?"

"A...uh...new preacher's family in Monticello. I can do it while you are working, so we won't be in your way."

"When I'm working? I work all day long. You are welcome to use the parlor. I assume you'll want those old drapes open. They are probably full of dust. I can shake them out this evening if you'll help me get them down."

"Huh?" Reg was away with some other thought. "Yeah, I can help with that. It won't be until next week sometime. It's for the Monticello paper, I think."

"That's fine. Do you want to go to the Grange Hall Saturday night for the dance?"

"Do a little jigging? Sounds aces to me. Want to practice right now?" He stood and held out his arms.

She laughed. "I have work to do. I say our jigging is as good as the next couple's. Please put your dishes to soak and I'll see you for supper." She got her gloves, hat, and lunch pail and shut the door behind her.

"Aces," Reg said as he walked into the dimly lit parlor and sat on the loveseat. He took a big drag on his cigarette and blew smoke rings into the air.

~

King stood in front of Sitton's bulletin board reading the news. He had read the year before about Hitler declaring himself the Supreme Commander of the German armed forces. Who was Hitler kidding? He was an monster trying to take over the world. King hated war and knew firsthand how it could change people forever.

He went outside to the store's big porch and sat in a rocking chair. The Battle of the Argonne Forest, in the Great War, was where he'd gone wrong in the head. He had read in *Life* magazine that over 26,000 American soldiers had died in that battle and nearly 96,000 were injured. He'd always wondered if that forest was lush and green before it was scorched to the ground and replaced with dead bodies for as far as a person could see. His hands trembled at the horrid sight that came to him night and day. He held tight to the arms of the chair.

That was twenty years ago, but the images, smells, and sounds of the forty-day battle had set up permanent camp in his brain. Now they'd posted that Hitler was building up his navy and putting troops on the border of Poland. Nobody but greedy supreme commanders wanted another World War, and they would steal the country's young men to fight their battles. There were times when he would like to poke a hole in his head and let that Battle out. He wanted to literally plant new trees where those men had sacrificed themselves. What was the point in him surviving anyway?

King was leaving the General Store porch when he saw Jenky drive by in his blue pickup truck. King took off his bandana headband and scratched his head, then put it back on. Jenky shouldn't have to be without a good woman like Violet Hendricks. It wasn't right no matter how you looked at the situation. It was all the fault of her pig-fearing, sissy man tenant. It was high time for that trash to be hauled off. King laughed at the first notion to pop into his mind. He did a short celebration dance, ending with a war whoop, and then walked over to the Grange Hall to see what was going on.

~

Jenky's voice echoed in the gymnasium as he extolled the benefits and joys of having electricity in the home and at the workplace, be it office or farm. He especially praised the power of electricity for the homemaker, both in the city and on the farm and he recognized the hard work and dedication of the local REA board. He inserted the "Power On, Colorado" phrase several times. By the end of his speech, Jenky could pause and the audience would interject it for him and at fever pitch.

When his speech was over, the public relations man for the Board took over to explain how the system would work and particularly how rural residents could get their homes wired to "power on". Jenky stayed until it was over and then shook hands with everyone he could. That was part of his job. A handshake, to him, meant, "*I am you* at the Colorado General Assembly and I will not forget that".

He drove to Dove Creek, thinking about Violet. She had never responded to his love letter. Either she loved this Repulsive Reg or she simply didn't care. He saw Reg coming out of the privy as he drove by her place. His initial reaction was to turn around and throw the man, headfirst, into the creek, but his better sense prevailed and he continued homeward. Once inside his house, Jenky carried all but one single calendar to the basement and loaded them into his grandmother's travel trunk. He still had the key to it. He locked the trunk and put the key away in a secret spot. He had no idea what he would do with them, but he knew what he would do with the solitary one upstairs.

Jenky wrapped the calendar in a couple of pages from the Rocky Mountain News, taped it in several places, and wrote her name on the front.

He knew they would go to the dance. Mr. Dancer-Prancer-Swindler-Romancer loved to perform too much not to attend. Jenky parked his pickup on the hill, out of sight from Violet's house. He saw Reg go to her back door and then the two of them left in Reg's car. Jenky waited a few minutes before rolling down the hill and into her driveway. He pulled right up behind the Maxwell, got out, placed the wrapped calendar on the driver's seat, and then left.

The Grange Hall was packed, smoke-filled, and overflowing into the street. Folks inside were hot already and the dancing had yet to begin. Lemonade and apple cider were being consumed. Jenky came in the side door to avoid seeing Violet and her date. He was introduced after the applause had died down, and then he gave the same speech he'd given in Cortez only with even more fervor because he saw Violet in the crowd. Afterwards, the public relations man gave the same information and answered questions.

Jenky went out the side door and waited for the music to begin. He paced the street in front of the Hall. He turned the corner and saw someone lurking around Reg's Roadster.

"Hey, who goes there?" he called out.

King stood up. "Jenky? It's me, King. How you doing?"

Jenky peered over King's shoulder. "Were you inside that car?"

"Naw, not really. I rolled up one of the windows so some good-for-nothings wouldn't mess around inside, it being so fancy and all."

Jenky studied King's face. "You are sweating like crazy, man. Why don't you go inside and have lemonade or cider?"

"I got my own stuff. Don't worry about me."

Jenky heard a grumbling noise. "What was that?"

King made a sound resembling a bullfrog. He blinked his eyes and held up his hands like claws, then laughed all the way to the front steps of the Hall.

Jenky wiped his own face with a handkerchief. He exhaled and followed King to the steps. Now or never.

The REA public relations man was just leaving in his car when Jenky went inside.

~

"How come you wore that braid tonight? It puts a damper on my style." Reg asked as they took a break.

Violet wasn't listening and couldn't help but look for Jenky in the crowd. He was so handsome tonight in his suit and tie. His speech was brilliant. She was ready to sign up for wiring right now.

Reg moved in front of her. "Hey, kiddo, I asked you why you wore your hair in a braid tonight?"

"Habit, I suppose," she said and spotted Jenky coming towards them. It took her off guard and she grabbed Reg's arm. "Let's dance."

They joined the others in a lively tune, but as Reg twirled Violet around, she saw Jenky approach them again. Maybe…no it couldn't be. He wouldn't try to cut in. Jenky said something, making Reg laugh. Then Jenky repeated the words. Reg said, loud enough for anyone nearby to hear, "I don't want to step outside. If you have something to say to me, do it right here."

Violet could not believe what happened next. Jenky raised his fists like a boxer and so did Reg, who was still cackling and calling Jenky names. Jenky swiftly cocked his arm, and then let his fist fly straight into Reggie's nose. It dripped blood immediately. Reg moaned and went to his knees. Jenky shook his open hand in the air several times, obviously from his own pain. He had barely started out the door when somebody in the crowd, it sounded like Tyrel Fetters to her, hooted and hollered and started clapping.

~

The applause and cheering were still going on as Jenky was pulling out of the parking space. He heard a familiar voice calling his name. He stopped.

Violet ran right to his window. Her eyes were wild and her voice shook. "Have you lost your marbles, Jenkins Butler? I am ashamed of you. You are supposed to be a leader and set an example for others. Now you've made a fool of yourself in front of everybody in this county. I never, ever want to see you again. The only vote you'll get next election will be your own."

Violet stomped off into the dark. Jenky waited until he could see her silhouette in the doorway of the Hall and then he was gone.

~

The Grange's social chairwoman, Nell Haggerty, who always wanted to be in the thick of things anyway, had attended Reg's nose injury with advice from a whole circle of busybody women. Most of them hadn't witnessed this type of excitement since grade school, if then. Violet and Reg moved towards the exit and the crowd resumed dancing with a fresh vigor. Those who preferred current events over dancing relived the glorious punching episode with varying degrees of accuracy but with magnificent enthusiasm and loyal admiration for Jenky.

~

Violet opened the passenger door and Reg scooted into the seat. He was certainly in no shape to get behind the wheel. She walked around to the driver's side. With her hand almost on the door, Violet recoiled as an unearthly sound erupted inside the car. It was Reggie. He screamed and screeched like a man possessed. He thrashed around making the car rock like a cradle. She was afraid to open the door. A small crowd gathered as more folks streamed out of the building to see what could be happening now on this night of nights. Some had brought lanterns from the Hall with them. A couple of take-charge guys were preparing to open Reg's door. His shrieks and squeals had many of the older ladies now pushing to the back of the crowd.

"On three," one of the men shouted.

The crowd, now game for about anything, began the count for them. At three, the men opened the door and Reg fell out. The crowd went silent, thinking he could be dead. It was then that two small, pink piglets, each about the size of a watermelon, tumbled out of the car and over Reg's limp body. Reg came to life, squealing and being squealed at by the pigs. King appeared out of nowhere and wrangled the babies into a gunny sack, then saluted the moon. Raucous laughter rippled through the crowd and continued as people milled around and gradually dispersed.

~

Violet comforted Reg as best she could on the way home. "It was probably some kids playing a joke, Reg. Word probably got around about that hog chasing you up the hill. You know how kids are."

He had stuffed the corners of a Grange kitchen dishrag inside his nostrils to help clot the blood, but making him appear to have a very dingy beard. His voice was nasal as a result. "Some joke. I could have died, especially after your old boyfriend belted me. I should sue him. He's rich, right? I have plenty of eyewitnesses." He rested his head on the back of the seat. "Do you smell manure?"

She did. "I'll clean it up. Vinegar and water will take the smell out."

"I'll sue those kids, too. This is an expensive car. *Jenkums* or whatever his name is, should buy me a new one. I'll get him kicked out of the Legislature. That's what I'll do. I know there's a newspaper in Denver. Probably two."

Violet drove up to the tack room door. "You get ready for bed. I'll bring you a clean cloth and water so you can wash up. I know you feel horrible now, but time heals almost everything. Get some rest. I am so sorry."

He headed straight for the privy. Violet pumped a small bucket of water and found a clean square of cloth in her rag bag. She filled a glass with water and set everything, including two aspirin, inside the tack room where he couldn't miss it. She lit his kerosene lamp and turned down his bed. Poor guy.

She went to the barn for a ditch digging shovel to clean out his car. His lamp was out by then. Her lantern revealed the back floorboard of the Roadster, and the deposits made by the two piggies. She shoveled out the mess and sanitized the floorboard with a vinegar solution. With the windows rolled down, it should be much improved by morning.

She cleaned her hands with soap and water, brushed her teeth, and went to bed. Bean curled up next to her. Violet's head buzzed with the evening's activities. She still felt the smoky heat, tasted the lemonade—sweet and sour, heard the band and then the laughing, cheering crowd as well as the squealing pigs, and she definitely smelled their piggy poop. Mostly, Violet could recall Jenky's fist plowing precisely into Reg's nose. It was puzzling and, sorry to say, a faintly amusing sight.

Why would Jenky have done such a thing? He had never fought physically with anyone, unless it was after he left Dove Creek. What a crazy night. She did giggle into her pillow thinking about those triumphant piglets taking a victory walk over Reg's chest. If she had the money to place a bet with someone as to whom they belonged, it would be on King. Those were his piglets and the joke was his doing. He was a big fan of Jenkums Butler. She giggled again.

⁓

Jenky soaked his hand in a bucket of cold water. Caesar decided to help himself to a drink from the bucket during the soaking process but Jenky didn't notice. He was thinking about Violet's words. He could see, from her perspective, that she might consider his punch to Reg's face as unprovoked and barbaric. He should have left the calendar somewhere else. What if Reg found it and Vi never saw it? Too late now for what if's. He would leave tomorrow. He had done what he could to make the love of his life aware of the danger in her tack room, and he had exacted a tad of western justice to the culprit's ego, if not his nose. He would have many hours on the ride to Denver to lament with only Caesar to offer consolation.

Chapter 10
Belated

By Wednesday, the swelling was down and the dark circles under Reg's eyes were more of a greenish color, almost the same as his eyes. He was joking around more and had taken two rolls of photos at the pool hall. Nobody there had dared mention the fisticuffs or the squealing piglets. Violet knew that, as soon as Reg had left the pool hall, the old timers had laughed their beards off and made many jokes at his expense. He seemed to think that all was well, which suited her fine.

After supper on Thursday, Reg was his old confident self. He smoked and watched her clean up. "Hey, dollface, there's a full moon tonight. What do you say we sit outside and watch it? Get in some real lovin', too. Let your hair down stuff."

Violet cringed at the word *dollface.* "I'm glad you brought up the 'real lovin' issue, Reg." She dusted crumbs into her hand. "Where are we going with all this? Is it a way to pass the summer or is it some form of dating? And what does my hair have to do with anything?"

Reg stubbed out his cigarette and pulled her into his lap. "What do you want this to be?" He kissed her.

That's how he liked to resolve issues, but not Violet. "I am not a school girl and I don't take love lightly. I can't see you settling down to life on a small farm on an even smaller budget, so I'm guessing that we are killing time until you get a new assignment and move on."

He kissed her again. "That's a crude way to put things. I'm not above making a married woman out of you, but you're right about me not being the rural type on a regular basis. I would be home and gone, here and away. I love action and I crave the city life. You know that I'm attracted to you more than anybody I've met before. If somebody could ever tie me down, it would be you, kiddo."

Tie him down? Violet searched Reg's face for a hint of emotion or devotion. She was either missing something or he wasn't offering much. She smiled. "Thanks for the compliment."

He lit another cigarette. "What are your plans tomorrow? Weed chopping all day?"

"Actually, not all day. I'll chop in the morning, but I need groceries, ice, and your rent money, please. In other words, I'll be in town in the afternoon."

Reg took out his wallet and gave her ten bills. "Tomorrow is the day I'm taking photographs of that preacher's family. Would morning or afternoon be better?"

Violet put the money in her apron pocket. "Haven't you already set the time up with them?"

He shrugged. "I told them to come by in the morning and if the time's not good, they will go visit with some local preachers in Dove Creek and come back in the afternoon."

She dipped the washed dishes into the rinse pan and then set them to dry on a clean tea towel. "Does this family have a name?"

He took a puff and appeared to be deep in thought. "I keep forgetting. I think it's Cheshire or Chester, something like that."

Violet saved the rinse water to be heated for the next meal's wash water. She tossed the current wash water out the back door. She wiped the dishpan dry and set it on the sideboard. Reg moved his feet so she could sweep under the table.

She put the broom away. "Morning should be fine. Like I said, I'll be chopping weeds."

"Uh...the preacher's wife said they would like for me to do some extra shots of their oldest daughter. I might be working on that at noon."

She shrugged. "I can eat my lunch in the field or I might go down by the creek to find a shade tree."

"Aces. If you don't want to watch the man in the moon with me, I'm calling it a night." He pushed back his chair and started for the back door.

"Good luck with the Cheshire or Chester family tomorrow."

"Who?" Reg asked over his shoulder.

"The minister and his family."

"Yeah, yeah. Thanks." Reg walked to the tack room, whistling a popular tune.

～

Violet got ready for bed, but thoughts of Jenky crowded her mind. She shouldn't have shouted that scolding like she did, but she still didn't know what the big punch was all about. When she repeatedly asked Reg about it, he had maintained that Jenky was a hot-tempered, jealous man. He wasn't hot-tempered at all but she wasn't sure about the jealousy accusation. Jenky had never been in a situation before to be jealous, so it could be that the punch implied he cared about her to some extent. That extent could have withered since her threats at the Grange Hall and at his house.

Violet gathered her nightgown around her and went to sit on the front steps. Bean purred then scampered off to chase a cricket. The moon was big and beautiful. Surely Jenky didn't believe that she never wanted to see him again. She wanted to see him right now. She closed her eyes and leaned against a porch post. He could have his arm around her and, since her hair was loose around her shoulders, he might move his hand along her neck and run his fingers through the wavy strands. Then, like she'd seen in the movies, she would lift her face to him and he would kiss her the same way he did that early morning. She opened her eyes. Swell. You've banished your one and only love from ever seeing you again. All of this heartache because you just had to take in a boarder. By the end of the summer, you will have thirty dollars to show for cooking and kissing with the wrong man. No amount of plumbing was worth that.

~

The next morning, after chores, Violet fried up some Johnnycakes and two slices of ham. She set out a jar of honey from Glenn and Bessie Stanley's beehives. Reg came in the back door and yawned loudly. She hated that. His hair was slicked back and he smelled of Bay Rum aftershave. He was wearing clothes she had never seen before.

She whistled. "You look sharp."

He was already eating. "I want to impress the preacher. Who knows? I could pick up a few bucks doing portraits on the side."

Violet sat across from him, then pushed her chair back. "Gosh. I forgot to shake out the drapes in the parlor. They need it, I'm sure."

He shrugged. "Don't worry about it. I'll take them down later. You have work to do." Reg put a tablespoon of honey on each of his Johnnycakes. "This ham is good."

"Thanks." Violet smiled. "It's from King's farm."

Reg stopped chewing and curled his lip at his plate. "The only good pig is a fried slice of ham, then."

At least he had a sense of humor and could out-dance anybody she'd ever known. For that matter, so did Mickey Rooney, but she wasn't in love with him either.

~

Violet didn't need the Farmall to transport her to the field today. She would be working in the area just on the other side of her barn. That's why she could easily take her lunch break on the infamous rocks where Reg had taken so many photos of her before the hog ran him off. Before leaving the farmyard, she filled her canteen with the cold, sweet water from her new well. As she screwed the lid on, it occurred to her that she hadn't been to town all week. The Maxwell could have chickens roosting in it by now. At least it should have plenty of gas to get her to the ice house and back later. She put on her big straw hat and work gloves.

∾

Violet checked her grandfather's pocket watch. Time for lunch and to call it a day. She slung her canteen over one shoulder, balanced the hoe on the other, and then picked up her lunch pail for the walk to the creek.

Dove Creek trickled along now, sometimes pooling around the rocks. It would swell with the next rainy season just before the first frost of autumn. Violet didn't sit on the rock where Reg told her to pretend she was lying in a field of flowers. Instead, she sat on a fallen log near the ponderosa pine stand. She liked to listen to the wind sighing in the trees. She and Jenky were toddlers when her papa had planted the pines. Later on, he had teased them about their children playing in the same shady spot, too. That prospect didn't seem too likely now.

She knew there was a word for their clashes. *Frustration.* That was crazy. If she hadn't been unbearably stubborn about taking on her parents' farm, their lives would have been more traditional. They would have courted in due time and then married, had babies that played in the shade of the pine stand, and gone on family trips to Denver and wherever else normal people went. Too late now.

Violet rearranged her belongings and plodded up the hill to her house.

∾

She didn't see any strange vehicles parked in the driveway—just hers and his, so she presumed the minister's family had come and gone. She put the hoe away and washed her hands at the pump. Bean greeted her with a lengthy purr. Violet didn't see Reg anywhere. She walked to the screened-in porch and removed her shoes and dusty socks. She passed through the kitchen and had to squint to see into the darkness of the parlor. Rather than being flooded with light from three windows, it seemed as though she was looking into a deep hole. Odd sounds were coming from the room. Violet did not move.

"Hello?" she said, and heard curse words flying as well as furniture creaking. She took a few steps towards one of the windows. Violet reached for the heavy drapery that her mother had bought to keep winter from seeping in. She jerked the curtain back. No need to search any further for Reg. He was in his skivvies with his arms out of the sleeves rendering him bare-chested. His hair stood like the quills of a porcupine and his eyes were little slits in the bright midday light. Those full lips were red with lipstick.

"Reggie! I thought you would be done with Mister...Reverend... Chest Hair...I mean Chester." She was obviously short-winded and dry-mouthed. "Who is that with you?" Violet pulled the curtain back all the way. On the loveseat behind Reg was a young woman in her late teens. Her bobbed, strawberry blond hair was a wreck and her mascara and lipstick were smeared. Her sleeveless blouse was halfway undone and her slim skirt was twisted sideways.

"Hi," the girl said, wrinkling her nose. "I was about to leave. Sorry." She giggled, picked up her high heels, and tiptoed out of the room, waving at Violet and whispering to Reg, "I'll be in the car."

He didn't even try to explain. Violet mechanically turned her attention to opening the rest of the drapes. Out of the corner of her eye, she saw him carrying his clothes and shoes out of the room. The screen door slammed and soon she heard more giggling and the Roadster rocketing away from her house.

～

Violet lugged and tugged until she at last relocated the loveseat to the front porch. It looked very elegant there, especially with Bean stretched out on it. She ripped down the drapes, wrapped them in a horse blanket, and then placed them into an old steamer trunk in the barn. She hauled the wheelbarrow to the tack room and loaded it with Reg's belongings, including his newsboy cap. She dumped it to the right of her mailbox. The second load, empty liquor bottles, she tipped out on the left. The third load she placed at the base of her mailbox, like so much fertilizer around a prize rosebush. She exhaled and returned to the tack room to remove and wash the sheets. As she pulled the mattress away from the wall, something fell behind the bed. Violet got on her hands and knees to reach it.

The envelope was tenderly addressed. ~**To my sweet Violet** ~ She touched the ink where it had been smeared with a stain. Gosh. Why hadn't she seen this before? Surely her former tenant wouldn't…oh, yeah, he would.

Violet didn't want to read it in the tack room. There was only one place for her to go. She walked to the creek again. The ponderosas were casting shadows now, so she sat on a nest of pine needles, outside the shade. She gently removed the letter. It was dated June 23, 1939, and was three pages long. Her throat tightened and tears were not far behind. And that was only after reading the date. Her heart ached as she read:

Dearest Violet,

How are you? (I want to start this letter correctly, as you mentioned.)

After all these years, I have decided, at last, that it is only fair for you to know what goes on in this foolish heart of mine. Any other man would have brought this up fifteen years ago. I suppose you could say that makes me a one in a million guy, but it's gotten me nowhere. I am lucky that you haven't been snatched up by someone else.

For reasons unknown, it is painful for me to share my feelings. But my time away from you is much more painful. I miss your beauty, grace, passion, wit, intellect, and fortitude as well as everything else about you. I miss sharing milestones and the smallest of things with you. Mornings bring a fresh new world, but all my days are framed only with your lovely image. Each meaningful thought includes a consideration as to what your perspective might be. So it seems you and I are together, even when we are apart. That does not work in theory, and it is nothing but torture in practice.

The idea has never occurred to me that I should consider another woman's attention. It has always and only been you for me, Vi. I think constantly about the twinkle in your deep blue eyes, your exquisite hair flowing around your shoulders, and your perfect lips smiling at me. If I were to be with you as your husband, I'd be kissing those lips all the time. Due to the amount of kisses, you might be denied simple sustenance and two-way conversation yourself, but never lacking in affection from me.

It would be my life's joy if we could be married, but I will not propose now. I shall do that soon, unless you don't respond in some way to this letter. First, we must kiss again, since it has been one heck of a dry spell for us in the romance department, as you well know. We have to rekindle the fire to give our grownup love a chance to burn with the same passion as our first love.

I truly believe that an intense passion—a certain longing, survives from our youth. I have always felt it when we touch. I carry that memory in my heart, as I live to touch you again. That's the honest reason why I love to slow dance with you.

Remember when we played Romeo and Juliet in our school play? I had no idea what Shakespeare meant with these words from the first act then, but now I know all too well:

> *Love is a smoke made with the fume of sighs,*
> *Being purged, a fire sparkling in lovers' eyes,*
> *Being vexed, a sea nourished with lovers' tears.*
> *What is it else? A madness most discreet,*
> *A choking gall and a preserving sweet.*

Any and all fault for our lonely, lovelorn circumstances rests with me, my darling Violet. I am the villain and the clown when I so wanted to be your hero.

With the greatest respect, affection, and all my love forever,
Jenky

Violet read it again and again. Reggie Magee should be put in jail for keeping this from her and stealing Jenky's precious words for his own pathetic purposes. It would be nothing but fair for her to accidentally burn his stuff by the mailbox. Who would blame her? She kissed Jenky's signature and bounded up the hill to the house. She would go to Denver and kiss him in person.

Violet was almost to the Maxwell when she heard Tyrel honking. He drove down the lane cackling and came to a stop no more than a yard away from her. She put her hands on her hips, holding tightly to Jenky's letter.

"Is Mr. Dreamboat getting the boot?" His mouth was frozen in a donkey grin.

She exhaled loudly. "Do I have mail, Tyrel?"

"Nope. So, has the smooth talker jigged his last jig?" More donkey grin.

Bean came out to rescue Violet. "Tyrel, you saw his things by the mailbox. They didn't get there by themselves."

Tyrel hee-hawed. "*Extra. Extra. Read all about it. Violet runs off another man.* That makes three of us men—me, Jenky, and now Mr. Marvelous Magee." He gunned his engine and made a quick, back-up getaway.

Violet hesitated in her response long enough for him to retreat. Three?

Tyrel was counting himself as one of her former beaus now. Gosh. He was crazier than poor old King for sure. She would rather kiss one of King's hogs than pucker up for Tyrel. How could his French wife put up with him? There was a chance that she still didn't speak English too well or that she needed glasses. Could be both.

～

Violet wasn't sure what to do next. Her Maxwell would have a hard time making the trip to Denver, but she had to go. Ethel would let her make a call to Jenky, but that wouldn't be the same as seeing him in person. She couldn't kiss him on the phone. Only one person in Dove Creek could tell her if the Maxwell was roadworthy and that was King. If it needed fixing up in a hurry, he could do it, if he liked you. He kept his own truck going when everybody else's was snowed-in with a dead battery. King's truck was a giant that he'd bought from the State of Colorado Highway Department when they bought new ones several years ago. It was a truck that he could attach a plow to in the winter and rescue folks if need be.

She scurried around the house and found an ancient, dusty valise that she could carry her essentials in and laid it open on her bed. The handle was about to fall off. But if she started on the trip today, she would spend most of it in the dark and nobody would see how pitiful her travelling necessities were. Wait. It might not be such a wise idea for a single woman to travel at night. It would be better to have King check out the car and leave in the morning. Settle down, Violet. The Maxwell didn't need anything major, surely. Ethel would know somebody who could do her chores for a couple of days.

She made sure Bean had water and that the Maxwell had gas, then she opened the door to get in. On the driver's seat was a square packet wrapped in newspaper and addressed to **Miss Hendricks** in a concise hand. Why would someone not send her whatever this was through the mail? Who would have been on her property and when?

She opened it and pulled out a calendar for 1940. The advertisement was for *Caesar's Deluxe Bath Fixtures*. She flipped to the first month and gasped at what she saw. She dropped the calendar. It was an extremely good drawing of her. She picked it up again and lifted each month to confirm the nightmare…twelve, life-like drawings of her were attached to each month. January was mild but by the time she got to December she had to hold on to the door handle. Her hands trembled and she had the urge to throw up. Who was *Caesar's Deluxe Bath Fixtures* and who put this in her car? Wait. Was that Jenky's printing on the envelope? She looked again. Of course it was. And who else would have a bath fixture store named Caesar's? Now she was confused about everything.

Violet resolved to look at the pictures again. This time she was angry by February. All of the drawings or paintings were the same poses that Reg had so precisely directed for his photographs. That she was sure of. The clothes were basically the same ones from his costume trunk, except December's model who wore nothing at all except a Santa hat. Where did that pose come from…unless Reg had peeked sometime while she was taking a bath! What a criminal he was. The sound of his camera clicking was in her brain, and it made her cheeks burn with embarrassment and unwarranted guilt.

Pacific Coast Calendar Company, Los Angeles, California, was stamped on the back of the calendar. It didn't matter who had made it or who had delivered the calendar to her. It mattered only that Reg the Reptile had somehow arranged to turn her photos into saucy pinup girls and apparently Jenky had seen them. Did he think she posed for Reg like the illustrations indicated? Horrors. He had to be told that Reggie had taken advantage of her. Hold it. That was not the best way to describe what had happened. Someone had based these pinup poses on her innocent photographs. How embarrassing that Jenky had seen those girls with her face looking right at him, many of them puckering up for a kiss. What a mocking gesture that would be for Jenky. How would this affect his respect for her? She lay across the seat and cried with shame that his eyes had seen her likeness in these compromising poses whether they were fact or fiction.

Violet took the calendar into the house, hid it under her collection of comic books which was tucked away with her nightgown, and then sat on her bed to consider her options.

She closed her eyes to picture Jenky walking towards her for the world's best kiss. That one had put all of her tenant's kisses to complete shame. A sound outside startled her. It could be that Reg was back. If she killed him and had to go to prison for the rest of her life, she would never marry Jenky. Better not do that. She went to the back door to see if his car was there. Instead of Reg's car, she discovered that it was pouring rain. The pinto beans could use a good soak. Just so it wasn't a flood. She closed the windows in the Maxwell, shut the chickens up, pulled the tractor into the barn, and brought Bean's food dish inside. It was still raining. Funny, she didn't notice any clouds when she was hoeing, but such was Colorado weather. It was a good time for her to think through this new catastrophe caused by her thirty-dollar tenant.

Now she knew why he wanted more and more photos. What other calendars were out there? She had to pay Reggie back for doing this or he would do the same to some other unsuspecting girl—perhaps the tittering person who was on her loveseat earlier in the day. Jenky could help her figure this out. The sooner she could get to Denver, the sooner she could kiss him and they could talk about how best to handle Mr. Magee.

The more it rained, the more convinced Violet became of a particular course of action. With great resolve, she went to her wardrobe, opened the drawer containing her socks. She nestled Jenky's letter inside and then felt around for a pair of Sunday gloves that had belonged to her mother. She stuffed one glove into a pocket of her overalls. Bean appeared in her doorway and meowed, letting her know that he wanted out.

Sure enough, the rain had slowed to a drizzle. Violet shut her back door as she left, wishing now that Jenky had installed locks. As she zipped the Maxwell up her lane, she happened to remember that all of Reg's belongings were piled around the mailbox. She got out to inspect them and was pleased to see that everything was soaked. His clothes, shoes, briefcase, suitcases, magazines, and his fancy hair toiletries were caked in Dolores County mud. It was disappointing that his photography equipment must have been in his sporty car because it hadn't been in the tack room. Too bad. She would have enjoyed seeing his livelihood go down the drain with the rest of the sludge.

~

"Violet, dear, it's so good to see you. How is Mr. Magee's nose?" Ethel asked quietly. Her hair glistened in the store lights.

"I wish it were broken, but it's not," Violet answered. "You will be glad to know that I have come to buy some dresses, Ethel."

"Is that a fact? You follow me and I will fix you up. How much do you want to spend? Remember you still have a credit balance from Jenky."

"Oh." Violet decided to tell her friend the truth. "I don't want to use that money today. I am going to see him in Denver and I am not wearing overalls to the Capitol. My problem is that I will have to buy gas to drive up there and back and possibly pay King to get the Maxwell in shape for the trip."

Ethel smiled. "You don't need to drive to Denver, Violet. Catch the bus over in Moab. It's a lovely trip when you don't have to drive it yourself. The bus takes you right downtown and you can walk to the Capitol Building. A round trip ticket is very reasonable."

Violet grinned. "That's swell. Surely the Max will make it to Moab." Violet reached for the glove and fished out a handful of one dollar bills and one ten. "Then I can spend half of this on clothes."

Ethel counted the money and gave twenty dollars back to Violet. "Between us girls, I'll pitch in five dollars and you can easily choose three dresses, shoes, and a purse. You'll need nylons, too."

Violet hugged her. "Thank you. I think I'm getting excited. Do you sell makeup? I need a new tube of lipstick."

"I have the perfect color. This will be fun. Do you have a suitcase?"

Violet shook her head, recalling the broken handle on what must have been her grandmother's valise.

"You can borrow mine. I'll run back to the house while you try these on. The dressing room is through there. Pauline can help you."

Violet glanced at the rack of dresses. She didn't remember ever buying a store bought dress. Even her funeral dress was sent from her aunt in Kansas.

Ethel saw the overwhelmed look on Violet's face. "Jenky will be thrilled to see you and I am so happy for both of you. You belong together. When I get back, you'd better have at least one dress picked out."

She drove home with three dresses, a pair of nylons, a garter belt, a pair of red shoes with an open toe, and new unmentionables. Two of the dresses were floral prints and the third was a solid navy. She couldn't wait to wear them with Jenky at her side.

She had an odd feeling that something wasn't right as she rounded the last curve before her place. When she saw that Reg's things had been removed from their muddy spot by the mailbox, she knew her intuition was correct. He was standing by his car and had parked in her regular spot next to the back door. There were no smiles exchanged between them. She was ready for a showdown.

Reg put out a cigarette and strode over to her car. He put his hands on either side of her door, like he was pinning her in. "You owe me half this month's rent and repayment for my property that you damaged without an eviction notice. I know the law." His brow was knotted up like a determined bulldog.

Violet pulled on the door handle and he pushed harder against the door. She maintained her poise. "If you will move away from my car, I can go inside and get what's coming to you."

Reg stepped aside and let her pass, but then he was right on her heels. She turned back and stared at him. He gave her a head start before trailing her again. He stopped at her bedroom door. Violet went to her wardrobe and took out the letter from Jenky and the hideous calendar.

"Come into the kitchen. I am not comfortable with you in my home anymore."

Reg took out another cigarette. "I don't really care about your comfort, *Mr.* Hendricks, but I do care about everything I own being put out in the rain. Now I'll have to replace the whole lot. How about you give me all my money back that I've paid you and we will call it even, although it's not."

Violet didn't want Reg grabbing the letter or the calendar. She stood with her back to the door so she could make a quick run for it, if necessary. "Mr. Magee, I am so pleased to say this to your face. You, sir, are an imposter, a liar, and a plagiarizer. I will pay you nothing because I'm almost certain you belong in jail." Violet's eyes were ablaze.

That choked him up, giving him a coughing fit. "I don't know what you are talking about, but if you're as smart as you think you are, you'd better pay up before I go to the sheriff."

"Perfect. I need to talk to him anyway." Violet squared her hips and leaned towards him like a mountain lion, ready to pounce. "What kind of lowlife does it take to steal someone's personal letter and try to quote it as though the words were his own?" Violet held out the letter briefly but then put it in her pocket.

Reg was surprised but not at all embarrassed. He laughed. "You can't do anything with that letter. That's not a good enough reason to withhold what's coming to me. The law would think you are a jealous old maid. Which you are."

"Hmm…" She unfolded the calendar to October, which was bad, but not as bad as December. "Wonder what the law would say about taking photos of an old maid, then without her permission, selling them to a calendar company who redoes them by gradually drawing the old maid with less and less clothing until she is only wearing a Santa hat?"

Reggie's ears turned red and he stammered around, claiming innocence. "Where did you get that? I don't know anything about a calendar. What proof do you have that I sold anything?"

"Maybe all those letters you signed for were paychecks. I know the law, too. If you used the postal service for fraudulent purposes, you are in bigger trouble."

Then he lunged at it. Violet instantly stepped out of his reach and he landed on the floor. He rose to his knees cussing and threatening her.

"Hey!" A voice at the screen door made them both jump. "Shut up and get out here," King shouted in his dog-scolding voice.

"Who, me?" Reg asked in a high-pitched tone.

King growled at him.

Reg did as commanded but with an attitude. "What do you want, crazy old man? Make it snappy." He kicked the door open and held it there.

King grabbed Reg's wrists and twisted them behind his back. Violet took the opportunity to hide her letter and the calendar under a stack of dishtowels. She edged her way out the door and watched as King herded Reginald past the Roadster and towards King's hog trailer.

"Take a look at Violet's new guard hog, mister. This here's the meanest, orneriest, and hungriest hog in Dolores County. Probably you aren't aware of this fact, but one big hog is better than two Dobermans when it comes to keeping undesirables like you away." King spat. "Get yourself an eyeful because the next time you see him will be your final day on this earth."

Violet snickered as Reg's eyes grew twice their size when he turned to see what fate awaited him in King's trailer. He blanched when he saw the hog.

"Now get outta Colorado, you boondoggler." King said and with one swift kick to his keister, sent Reg on his way. Reginald Magee didn't dare look Violet's direction as he jumped in the Roaster and sped off.

King did an imitation of Reggie's reaction combined with one of his signature dances. He motioned for Violet to come to his trailer. "You gotta see my new boar. I bought him today in Monticello."

She stood on the trailer hitch and looked in the trailer at a giant sleeping hog. "Good grief, King. How much does he weigh?"

"About as much as a locomotive, I reckon. I got him from a fella over there that was asking me about your renter. He says that his teenage daughter is in love with him and they're gonna run off together. They've been courting for a couple of months. I told him that Mr. Hollywood was nothing but a worm in the muck as far as I knew. He said he reckoned that himself. I took a notion to come by and check on you, seeing as how my hogs were the reason you nearly died. But then I saw that rat-faced fella's car and came on down. He was up to no good, exactly as I would expect from a twit."

Violet thanked him and gave King a hug. He removed his bandana headband and twirled it while he hopped around like a rabbit, and then hollered so loud that the boar stirred and wobbled the trailer as he came to life. She laughed hard with King, but in her heart, she would always be grateful to this loyal, caring, and extremely strange man. He saluted her and left in his big truck.

～

She was awake long before dawn to get her chores done. Pauline and her husband, Raymond, who both worked at Sitton's, would be doing the chores for her. Violet heated water for her bath as she laid out her clothes. Bean watched from the edge of her bed. Everything else was packed in her borrowed suitcase.

Violet chose the dress with tiny blue flowers on a cream-colored background. She would wear her red shoes with it and her new purse. She washed her hair with Halo Shampoo from Sitton's, and hoped Jenky would notice.

～

Wednesday morning, at six o'clock, she gave Bean a good petting and filled his water dish. Pauline and Raymond would take good care of him for as long as she was gone. She loaded the Maxwell, put Jenky's letter in her purse, and drove away towards Moab. Her hair flowed down her back like a coffee-colored waterfall.

～

After a bumpy ride on the dirt road from Dove Creek, Violet parked her car near the Moab bus depot, unloaded her things, and walked to the station. She put her hand on the doorknob and twisted. The door didn't open. She set her hip against it and pushed. Nothing. Then she saw the sign and her heart sank.

> **Days of service –**
> from North and East – *Monday*
> to South and West – *Tuesday*
> from South and West – *Thursday*
> to North and East – *Friday*
> **Closed** Wednesdays and weekends.

She covered her mouth and sat on her suitcase. Why didn't she check on the bus schedutle before she drove over? What an idiot. Now she would have to wait until Friday to travel, and there was no telling where Jenky would be on the weekend. She would need more gas money.

An skinny, older man came out of the café next door. He was wearing a butcher's apron and a little white cap. "You are hurt, Miss?" He had an Italian accent.

Violet wiped her eyes with her knuckles. "Just my pride. But thanks. I drove over from Colorado to take the bus to Denver without checking the schedule. I'm an idiot."

He bobbled his head. "We see that all the time. No thinking you are the idiot or you are only one to do this. "You like some breakfast, *sí*? Come in—no charge. I will tell my wife."

Violet followed him like a puppy. The café was simply furnished with mismatched tables and chairs. He led her to a small table with a checkered cloth spread over it. The man told his wife something in Italian. She smiled warmly and brought coffee.

There were two other customers eating and talking. The old man must be the owner and the cook, Violet thought. His wife was large, with a round face and kind eyes. Her English was better than his.

She set a plate of fruit and a pastry in front of Violet and said, "Sorry you are upset, dear. Food will help soothe your worries. More coffee?"

Violet was expecting eggs and bacon. "This looks very good. I would like more coffee, please." She took a bite out of what seemed to be a doughnut without the hole. It melted in her mouth with a center filling that tasted like a cross between cake icing, raspberries, and heavy whipped cream. It didn't make her feel better. It made her think she was in pastry heaven.

She drank her coffee and then went to the register where the Italian lady was making change for the other customers.

The woman put her hand up towards Violet. "No charge to put a smile on someone's face. The schedule for the bus is *pazzo*—you say crazy. It is a...small potatoes operation from Denver, so they have to make the most of their buses. They only have two little ones and the drivers sleep in them before driving back to Moab."

The skinny cook came alongside his wife. "You like the *bombolona*? I see you were licking your fingers, no?"

Violet laughed. "Yes, I was. It was delicious. Thank you for cheering me up. I have to get home now and make new plans."

The man handed her a small brown bag. "You take more home. If it's trouble with *vero amore* calling you to Denver, then you will need more *bombolonases*."

His wife giggled in agreement. "He said that if it's trouble with true love, you will need more of the pastry."

"Goodbye." Violet blushed and put the brown bag in her suitcase.

Arrivederci, they said in unison.

～

It was raining by the time she got to Monticello, Utah. The road from there to Dove Creek had already been washed out from the major storm when she got sick. It was a washboard. Now, in this slow but steady rain, she had to dodge big holes and gullies that were hard to see in advance due to the poor condition of the Maxwell's old windshield wiper. At one point she was driving too fast and hit a gully hard enough to make the chassis bounce, twist, and come back down like a clap of thunder. She had to restart the engine. It took a few times to get going again but something was not right. The Maxwell crept along the muddy road. The rain blurred visibility of everything. If she could just make it to a house, maybe they could tow her home. It wasn't much farther to Dove Creek. That thought had no more than flickered in her head when a freight truck came barreling right into her lane. She ran off the road and into the borrow ditch.

∽

Almost two hours later, Violet slogged up the steps of Sitton's store. The rain had begun to taper off. Her Maxwell was left behind while she walked the rest of the way in the rain, wearing her floral blue dress and red shoes. She looked as though the *Bride of Frankenstein* had emerged from a muddy swamp.

Ethel was the first to notice her. "Lord have mercy, Violet. What happened to you? Did the bus have a wreck?"

Everyone in the store crowded around. Pauline handed her a towel with the price tag still on it. Howard guided her slowly to the pot-bellied stove and into a rocking chair. She told her tale of woe about the bus, the road conditions, the Maxwell's wiper, the freight truck running her off the road, and her long, grubby, wet walk into town.

Ethel was mortified that she herself hadn't called to check on the bus schedule. "I knew it had changed hands a few months ago and folks weren't happy with the new owners. I am so sorry, Violet."

Howard put on his sweater. "I'll run over to King's place and see if he can tow in your car and repair it." He patted Violet's damp shoulder. "Things will work out, have patience."

∽

Violet was sent to the Sitton's house behind the store to clean up and change into dry clothing. She returned wearing an old dress and wool sweater of Ethel's and a pair of rubber boots. Her hair couldn't possibly smell like Halo Shampoo anymore and her new stockings were full of runs, holes, and caked with mud. They were in the wastebasket now. She would give anything to start the day over.

∽

Ethel spoke with hesitation. "Now, Violet, I know you probably won't like this idea, but I have to suggest it. Call him. You could at least talk things out. I just know that Jenky will be down here in a flash."

Violet offered a weak smile. "Thanks but I need to see him when I tell him how I feel. Are the shoes ruined?"

"We're working on that, dear. Your dress might be presentable after it's ironed. I washed it and we have it hanging in the storeroom."

Before Violet could offer to iron her own dress, the front door opened with a bang and in walked King.

He was not happy. "Violet Hendricks!"

She raised her hand like a schoolgirl. "Yes. Over here."

"Are you hurt?" He came within inches of her face and looked her over.

Violet smiled at his intensity. "I'm all right, King. How's the Maxwell?"

He did a quick dance to celebrate her well-being, then he stopped. "Why didn't you wait in the car? I know you were valedictorian of your class."

"I did wait for a while, but the rain kept coming and I thought the Craig place was just ahead, but I must have already passed it."

He paced around the hardwood floor, leaving muddy footprints. "Nobody stopped to help or offer a ride?"

Violet raised her brow. "Are you chewing me out? I was afraid to walk on the road, since a truck almost hit me, so I walked in the ditch. Besides, there weren't many people driving around in a storm."

King pointed at her. "Except Violet Hendricks. You weren't out lookin' for that no-good renter, were you?"

Violet's face reddened. "I most certainly was not. I was trying to get to Denver to see Jenky. Can you fix my car or what?"

He saluted. "Going now to look for a part in my collection. See you later, ma'am. Hello, Howard and the missus." King turned like a soldier and marched out the door.

Ethel snickered and Violet joined in.

"Poor fellow," Ethel said between giggles.

Howard had to chuckle, too. "Say what you will, but nobody fixes engines and automobiles like King."

Violet rubbed her temples. "He's right. I should have waited in the Maxwell. I wasn't thinking straight. The truck incident really jangled my nerves."

Ethel slipped her arm around Violet's slender waist. "It's been a long day, dear. You are welcome to stay here tonight or Howard can take you home. Right, honey?"

Howard nodded dutifully.

"Thank you for everything, but I should go home. Could I iron my dress first?"

"Nonsense. I'll plug in the iron and set up the board. Won't take five minutes. You get yourself a Coke out of the refrigerator and try to relax."

Violet went out on the porch to drink her icy cold Coke. Ah, the comfort of electricity. Customers nodded her way, probably wondering who died since she was wearing a dress again. Why did this mess have to happen, just when she was so happy and hopeful that all would be well soon. Did God not want her to go to Denver?

Ethel came out with the dress. "It looks better, not new, but almost."

Violet saw that there were stains on the skirt. "Thank you, Ethel. I'll change into it and give your clothes back. Could I borrow these boots? I'll bring them by as soon as the Maxwell is fixed."

"You keep all that," Ethel said as she rocked in a chair next to her. "That stuff is older than the hills. I'd better get back inside, Pauline has her hands full. Here are your shoes." She set a brown paper parcel in the rocker.

~

The sun came out and warmed her weary bones. She changed into her ironed, mud-stained dress. Violet did not like depending on the kindness of others. She alone had made the mistake of walking into town in a downpour and ruining her clothes. She should walk home. Gosh. She had left Ethel's suitcase in the Maxwell. Surely nobody would steal it. Besides, King had her car at his place now. She rocked in the chair and fell asleep.

She dreamed she was on the bus as it had wound its way through stunning passes with monstrous drop-offs that ended in a miniature river below. Violet was driving. But then she was a passenger and had contended with a chatty Italian woman, and twin little boys who insisted on taking turns sitting in her lap while they ate melting chocolate bars. Violet's dress was wrinkled and had smudges of Hershey bars on the skirt. She woke up to wolf whistles from a clump of teenage boys watching her sleep while they shared a Hershey bar. She must have smelled the chocolate to put it in her dream like that or heard the distinct rattling of the wrapper.

Violet smiled at the silly boys and went inside, carrying the parcel Ethel had left. She found Pauline and told her she wanted to walk home. It was only a couple of miles. She had already walked that far in the rain.

Pauline bit her lip. "Ethel won't like it, but I'll tell her. Violet, my Ray says for you to keep an umbrella in your car."

Violet nodded and headed for home.

~

The air was crisp from the rain and the rubber boots let her walk on the muddy road through puddles, like a little girl. The sun shone through the bright green of the refreshed plants and trees. A chorus of birds chirped in the cottonwoods and she saw more than one rabbit hide behind sagebrushes as she made her way. A meadowlark sang his own lovely solo from a pasture. She could listen to that sweet song all day. Her house came into view, bringing her charming, pastoral sensations back to reality. She was still in Dolores County, longing to be with Jenky, and he was still in Denver, thinking she didn't love him.

Violet took off the boots inside her screened-in porch. Bean was glad to see her. There were chores to be done since Pauline and Raymond knew quite well that she was still home. She changed into her overalls but wore Ethel's rubber boots to the barnyard. They would do well for mucking the cow stall.

~

She had just gathered eggs when King arrived in his giant truck that always sounded like a stampede of large mammals in a cowboy movie.

She shaded her eyes from the evening sun. "Hello there. Any luck with the Maxwell and did you find a suitcase in it?"

King removed the bandana from his head and gave his hair a run though with his fingers. "Could be that I'm gonna give you bad news and it ain't about your suitcase. That part's fine."

She seemed destined to get nothing but bad news. "Go on, let me have it."

"That car has a serious problem. I can go into the details for you, but it ain't gonna change the facts."

Violet lurched into a brief, but impressive crying jag.

King stepped back with saucer eyes. "What can I do to help, missy? I'm awful sorry. Here, let me take the eggs for you." He set the egg bucket on the ground and Violet put her arms around his neck as he leaned over. He couldn't stand up nor squat down with her arms like that. He hadn't been hugged in years. So, he stayed bent over until she finished crying.

Violet wiped her face on her shirtsleeves. She was quiet for an awkward minute, then cleared her throat. "I wonder if you would mind driving me to Moab Friday morning, King?"

"You gonna try to catch that fool bus again? It's still snows on some of them high passes. Buses ain't good on snow, even with chains on."

"I have to talk to Jenky. He may not be around over the weekend. The bus won't get there very early, but I'm willing to take the chance. Will you take me to Moab?"

King stared at the egg bucket for a few seconds. "No. But I'll take you to Denver."

She put both hands over her heart. "In your big truck?"

"This used to be a Colorado Department of Highways truck. All four wheels pull it along and it has a snowplow if we need it on top of Wolf Creek Pass."

"Wolf Creek Pass? I didn't know all of that road was finished. Are you sure it's okay?"

"We could leave right now. I'll tell those good-for-nothings to take care of my place for a few days. I can sleep in the truck in Denver. Not sure if I'm ready for big-city driving. You might have to figure the downtown part out on your own, but I'll get you as close as I can, safe and in one piece."

"You're saying you'll drive all night." Violet closed her eyes. This was a downright scary prospect but she had no better alternative. She had to talk to Jenky. "Okay, but all the money I have is the price of a bus ticket from Moab to Denver. You can't drink. And no cigars."

King clapped his hands scaring Bean to seek cover under the wheelbarrow. He suddenly saluted Violet. "Not to fret about my driving at night. Sometimes I go for days without sleep. Price of combat. I have to get rid of my trash collection in the back and put on my traveling duds. I'll be back later. No need for money to exchange hands. I'm playing Cupid for two fine folks." He saluted again. "No booze and no lighting up." He stepped up into the truck cab and backed all the way to the county road, singing *Camptown Races,* for some unknown reason.

Violet stood in the shadow of her barn and wondered what she had just done.

～

She opened the parcel to see if her muddy shoes were wearable at all. As she folded back the last bit of brown paper, she caught her breath. They weren't the shoes she had worn in the rain; these were an identical, unworn pair with brand new stockings tucked inside each toe. *That sweet Ethel.* She would pay for the replacements when she came back.

∽

Violet packed Ethel's sweater and the red shoes into the old valise and decided to wear Ethel's rubber boots in King's truck. What if it reeked of hog manure and she smelled the same way by the time they arrived in Denver? What if King drove off the road going up and over the Wolf Creek area mountains and she never saw Jenky again? It was a frightening pass on both sides, that, as far as she knew, didn't yet connect at the summit—much less have a hard surface to drive on. *Oh, Lord, have mercy. Lots of mercy.* She meant that with all due reverence.

∽

The sun was setting when King returned. He had changed into an ill-fitting, wool suit that looked as though goats had chewed on it and was sporting a fedora—with what appeared to be a bullet hole in the crown. His shirt was similar to one that her papa was buried in, but he seemed proud to have surprised her with his change of attire. The truck didn't smell too disgusting. In fact, it smelled more like Reggie than she would have preferred. Her borrowed suitcase separated the two of them on the front seat.

"I took the liberty of buying us a few candy bars and Coca-Colas for the journey. They are in that box in the floorboard. There's an opener in there, too," King said as they pulled onto the state road. "I also told the Sittons our plans. The missus was not thrilled about it, but she said Pauline and Raymond would take care of your place, as planned, and that she would pray for our safe travels. Hope it's okay with you that I took it upon myself to inform them. They are good people."

Violet could only imagine Ethel's reaction, but then King was trying to take care of business. "Sure. You have such good manners when you want to show them."

"I have good grammar, too, when I want to show it. I like to throw in bad grammar to expand my reputation as a nut case—like the dancing and hollering. It keeps me at a distance from meddlesome people. Did you notice that the back is all clean and tidy?" he asked.

Violet turned in her seat. "I have never seen it look better."

He pointed to the floorboard of the cab. "Notice I scraped most of the pig mess off my floorboard. Hope your boots are clean. I wasted half a bottle of whiskey on it to kill the germs, seeing as how you already had to contend with my pigs' muck in your recent health scare."

So that's why the smell reminded her of Reg. Violet turned her head so King wouldn't see her giggling. Hopefully, it would air out soon.

~

The truck was so noisy, they rode in silence to Durango where King stopped at a filling station for gas.

"I like to keep it close to full and not close to empty," he explained.

"Me too," Violet said with a bite of Hershey bar in her mouth.

King patted his belly. "I feel the same about my stomach, so can you fish me out a couple of Baby Ruth bars?"

Violet reached into the box again. They pulled away towards Pagosa Springs eating chocolate, drinking Cokes, and shouting conversation over the engine.

"Do you know who Baby Ruth bars are named after?" King asked, picking a morsel out of his beard.

She shook her head.

"Grover Cleveland's daughter." King watched her reaction.

"Really. I thought maybe it was named in honor of Babe Ruth. How do you know that?"

He bit into his second bar. "I remember things I learned before the war. Not much since."

"Were you drafted?"

He saluted. "Yes, ma'am."

"How old were you?"

"Just shy of my thirtieth birthday."

"Were you married?"

He didn't respond, so she was quiet for awhile. She fell asleep and woke up in Pagosa Springs at another filling station.

"Rest stop." King opened his door. "Long road ahead."

Violet went to the ladies' room behind the station. The evening was chilly and the facility even colder. She got the sweater out of the valise and climbed into the truck. Next was Wolf Creek Pass. King inspected his engine and the tires as well.

On the road, he sang old songs. Violet joined him in "You are My Sunshine".

He sniffed. "My wife's name was Daphne and she was a beauty." He whistled. "She died in childbirth, along with the little one."

Violet looked away. She considered how King's life had changed from the way he might have envisioned it. Certainly he hadn't planned for his wife and baby to die. And he couldn't have known that the actions of leaders in Europe would cause him to travel across the ocean and be surrounded by unspeakable horror. Her whiny complaints about life without electricity and indoor plumbing were ridiculous compared to what soldiers had endured. No wonder King had issues.

"What were your parents like?" She reached for another Hershey bar, a Baby Ruth and opened the last two Cokes for them. A light rain trickled down the windshield. He turned on the wipers. They moved reluctantly, due to the slow speed of the truck. "My folks were odd. I think I disappointed them by studying law. Not sure what they expected of me. They had money. Wanted to appear like Bohemians but they weren't. My grandpa on my mother's side was a serious big shot in the steel business."

He paused and looked her way. "Just between you and me, before the War, I was a lawyer...a good one, too." He waited for her to react but she was quiet. "After the war, I was in a sanatorium for quite a while then I went west to work at Mr. Butler's steel mill over in Pueblo, even though he didn't live there anymore. His father knew my grandpa. When the big flood came to Pueblo, it was too much like a war zone for me to handle. I followed Jenky's dad over to Dove Creek and did odd jobs for him and he set me up in the pig business—gave me the land. I owe the Butlers for taking care of me. They were good people, too. Real good people, like your Jenky."

She smiled, but was still stuck on King being a lawyer. "Did you like being a lawyer?"

"Sometimes it warmed my heart to help people that needed it. Way too much paperwork and long hours, though. I like the outdoors. Soooo-eeeeey!"

Just then a doe and two spotted fawn came up in the headlights. King stayed calm, slowed down, and the deer took off running.

"Dang. I always thought my hog calling was powerful, but I never knew it called up deer."

Violet laughed and noticed that snow had collected on the road. "Are we coming to the scary parts?"

He guffawed. "It's all scary, missy. Haven't you seen it?" He turned on the heater.

"No. I was supposed to go to Denver when I was little, but I got sick."

"You take another nap then. You'll either wake up in Heaven or Del Norte. I bet you didn't know that when Del Norte was a boom town, it was runner up to Denver to become the state capital. Lost by one vote." He then concentrated on the road because the snow was coming faster and with bigger flakes as they seemed to make a U turn.

Violet peered out the side window. "What are you doing? Are we turning around?"

"Just a hairpin curve. Lots of trucks fly right off the mountain here. It helps that we are going up rather than down. I'll check the brake oil when we get to the summit."

She closed her eyes. Great. She was riding in a giant truck moving into a high-altitude snowstorm with King Lewis at the wheel, negotiating hairpin curves, and possibly flying off the mountain. Every girl's dream come true. Pray extra, Ethel.

The worst part was when Violet couldn't see anything but snow out her window. Or maybe that was best. King had been extolling stories of the sheer cliffs along this side of the Pass. Could he make this any more worrying?

King sat up straighter behind the wheel. "This here is what's known as a white-out or a blinder. Being a Colorado girl, I reckon you know about that. Hold on to your seat, Violet Hendricks. Do the Lord's Prayer or that part of the twenty-third Psalm that talks about walking through the shadow of death."

"What?" It came out very sharp.

He glanced at her. "I'm only giving you a job to keep your mind off the danger. You should be thanking me." He had saucer eyes himself.

She gulped and prayed. The truck went maybe a foot sideways but King didn't flinch. Violet figured their speed at 5 mph. There was no possible way to see anything and nowhere to stop. Her heart drummed in her ears.

King squinted ahead, looking for vehicles and insane drivers that might be on the road. "We are nearly to the top, I think. I'll pull over when we're there and let this blinder lose some power."

Yes, Violet knew about blinders—snowstorms that gave no hint of objects or shadows. How King thought they were at the top, she did not know. Maybe they were traveling faster than she thought.

King pointed at her window. "Crank that down and tell me when you see what might be a pullout."

"A what?" She began cranking. "I can't see anything." She wanted to add *are you crazy*? But...

"Watch for a break in the level of snow. It hasn't been snowing all day.

This is a flurry. There's usually a wide spot or a pullout at the summit of a pass. I know where we are."

Her hair and face were showered with big flakes. "Wait, wait. I see what you mean. Maybe right here. I'll get out and check."

King rolled to a stop. "Watch your step."

Violet tugged at the wool sweater and shuffled to the side. She could see that it wasn't a sudden drop for at least eight feet, so she scooted a little more. Extra room there, too, and ahead of them. One more shuffle and there was still hard-packed snow.

"I think this is a good place, King," she shouted. "Be careful." Something shadowy caught her eye.

He reversed a few feet and pulled into the spot like a hand in a glove. She shivered and climbed inside the warm cab.

"Gosh, King. I think I saw something back there." Violet was backwards in the seat with her face against the window. "You have to see what it is. I'd say ten feet behind us in this pullout."

King frowned and took a flashlight from under his seat. He made his way to whatever it was and yelled at her. "It's a car and there's a man in it. He's alive, I think. Open your door."

Violet moved quickly. She got out just as King materialized from the darkness. She set Ethel's suitcase on the snowy ground. King's hair and beard was covered in snow, and the man he carried looked dead to her.

King stuffed the limp fellow into the cab and covered him with his wool suit coat. "He's trying to talk. See if you can hear him. I'm going to get some signal lamps out of my tool chest so we won't get slammed into."

Violet went to the driver's side, slipping once and landing on her derrière, but managed to crawl in close to the man's head. He shivered. She leaned so near him that his faint breath was warm against her ear.

"Need food," he whispered. "Diabetic."

She rocked back. Food. Candy. She felt around for the cardboard box and reached inside. It was empty. She backed out of the cab and got her footing on the ground.

"King! This guy might be having an insulin shock episode or something. Is there more candy or soda or water somewhere?"

King walked to the open door and stared at him. "No more nothing. We ate it all."

"Perfect." Violet gathered a handful of snow and held it while she scrambled into the cab. She held her fist over his partially open lips and let the bit of melting snow drip into his mouth. "God help us." She knew about diabetes from a detective story. "King, do you have anything that would serve as a cup?" Her hand was freezing cold.

He was no help. "A cup? Naw. I cleaned this thing out so you would travel in style."

"This guy won't make it if we don't do something now. I know—break a Coke bottle in half, then fill up the bottom part with snow. Hurry. He needs sugar, though."

King went to work slapping bottles against the rear bumper. He reappeared with a jagged cup full of snow. Violet held it near the heater vent, then kept up her drip process.

She had a brainstorm. "Can you do this for a minute? I need something out of my suitcase."

Reluctantly, he took over. Violet shuffled to the other side, opened her suitcase, and took out the brown bag that held the *bombolonases*, brought along purposefully to make things better.

And they did. She fed the man bits of the pastry and melted snow as they inched down the other side of the pass and found a hospital at Del Norte.

Violet understood now. All the delays and setbacks were leading to that precise moment on Wolf Creek when someone's prayers would be answered by an unlikely pair in a snowplow truck with empty Coke bottles and bombolonases. She smiled up at the stars. Mysterious ways, indeed.

Chapter 12

The Enchantment

*T*here it was—the gold leaf dome. Violet pointed out the historic site but King did not take his eyes off the traffic light. The last thing that Howard Sitton had said to her before she'd left for the infamous Moab bus station was, "You can't miss the dome. It is gilded with gold leaf to mark the importance of gold mining to our state."

King moaned. "I have to park somewhere fast or I'm gonna start yelling. It's coming over me, missy. The night driving, that half-frozen man, and this traffic is getting to my head."

She took him seriously. "Okay. There's a parking space under that tree. See it?" She pointed towards the spot.

"Nope. I need one at the end of a block. My truck is bigger than these little toy cars."

"Gotcha. There's an end space on the next block. Will that one work?"

"Yeah. Here we go." King twisted and turned the steering wheel perfectly. He killed the engine and laid his head on the back of his seat. Violet put on lipstick, using her new mirrored makeup compact.

King raised up. "Not to embarrass you, but I was real impressed with the way you saved that young man's life, Violet Hendricks. You deserve a boy scout badge for your quick actions. He thinks so too, along with all the doctor and nurses at that hospital. I don't remember the fellow's name, but he'll remember yours. Somebody said that he's a reporter at the Denver Post."

Violet blotted her lips. "I didn't know that, but you are the one who saved him. You drove through a blinder, found him, and carried him to safety. Now you rest in the truck and I'm going to the Capitol. I can't thank you enough for bringing me all this way. What a night."

He saluted.

Violet reached for the door handle but changed her mind. "I want to tell you a secret, King."

He opened one eye. "Shoot. I'm listening."

She motioned for him to lean over. When he did, she kissed his cheek.

He turned stoplight red. "Hey, get out of my truck, and I'm not leaving until you show up here on Jenky Butler's arm."

Violet changed shoes and left with her suitcase.

King lay all the way across the seat and closed his eyes. Maybe he was spared in France to help rescue somebody on Wolf Creek Pass. That would be worthy, sort of like planting a tree in a burned out forest.

～

Violet took a seat on a park bench to recompose her plan. So much had happened since she had decided to look him in the eye and state her case. Her mind careened at the notion that Jenky was so at hand now. She eyed the stately and beautiful Capitol. But she was not here to marvel and sightsee. She was here to proclaim her love. But what if he wasn't in his office today? What if he didn't want to see her?

Jenky had never said a word about her not getting to go with his family to Denver that time when they were kids. Instead, he had brought her back a rock he'd found in Elitch's parking lot. He left it in a little jar at their secret spot by Dove Creek. He could be that way...sort of mysterious.

How silly of her, knowing Jenky the way she did, to think he was going to make the first move in their longtime romance. She had his letter in her purse. Now if she could only remember which way Ethel had told her to turn after she got inside the Capitol to freshen up.

～

Sweat beads had collected on her forehead by the time she arrived at the ladies room. It might have been easier if she had asked for directions, but she was determined to find it on her own. She opened the suitcase and chose the navy dress. It didn't show the creases as badly as the other one. She stumbled around and put on the stockings, slipped back into her new shoes, brushed her hair and closed the suitcase.

She practiced walking in the heels and then stopped at the mirror. *The Bride of Frankenstein* was gone but she could still easily pass as her cousin. Her hair was loose and down, seeing as how it was so important to Jenky, but it looked like a mop. The seams in her stockings were crooked, too. Oh, well. Too late for primping, as though she knew how. Time for action. Violet unwrapped a stick of gum and hoped it would work magic on her breath.

～

She entered the main portion of the Capitol building and stood in awe at the rotunda, the white marble floors, the magnificent carved wood, the rose-toned marble wainscoting, and the stained glass windows. It reminded her of cathedrals she had seen in magazines and encyclopedias at school. So this was where Jenky worked. It was somewhat grander than a barn and an outhouse.

Violet asked the location of Representative Butler's office, and the prim lady behind the desk informed her that Jenky wasn't in his office. She gasped at the news. But he *was* presently in an emergency committee hearing.

"Where does the committee meet?" Violet asked, clutching her suitcase tighter.

The woman looked her over, including the suitcase. "Is there something I could help you with? Are you from his constituency?"

"Yes," Violet said, thinking fast, "I am testifying before the committee."

The lady raised a brow in suspicion, but gave in to Violet's sweet smile. "Follow me."

They walked down a long, marbled hallway. The lady stopped beside a door and held her finger to her lips to shush Violet. She opened the door and pointed to a back seat behind a tall man taking notes.

Violet seated herself and set the suitcase at her feet. Her heartbeat pounded. There he was, her dearest Representative, absorbed in a question he was asking of the person testifying about laws for train crossings or something. What an important job he had. How handsome he was in his suit, vest, and tie.Representative Edward Jenkins Butler was definitely more handsome than the man shaving in her Sears catalog illustration. Best of all, Jenky was a good man. No, he was the very *finest* man with a good and generous heart. She wanted to run to the front of the room and kiss him at that very instant. Instead, she swallowed her gum.

She'd better wait and not do anything too spontaneously romantic. But she did want to surprise him like he did her the morning he left. Now it was his turn to be holding the milk bucket and the lantern. He would certainly drop them both during *her* kiss. She had something like that in mind only it was on his territory. The air in this room was electric, like right before lightning struck a dead tree near her when she was seven. Or it could just be her heart going crazy.

Violet was peeking around the man in front of her when Jenky said, in a booming voice, "The Committee thanks all of you for your testimony and co-operation in this matter. We hope to get the bill written as quickly as possible and submitted for immediate passage in both houses. This committee is adjourned."

The roomful of people began talking at once to one another. Violet took it as a signal for her surprise. She spied Jenky being cornered by several important-looking men. She closed her eyes and imagined him walking towards her with that determined, steely look in his eye, at least as far as she could see then, in the light of dawn. That same determination was in her at this moment. She shoved her suitcase aside and strode towards the group surrounding him.

"Representative Butler!" Violet shouted as she neared him. The men turned towards her, leaving a clear path to Jenky. Her pulse quickened and his eyes widened.

"Vi?" he said, dropping a file of papers.

"Do you have time for a loyal constituent?" she asked quietly, then slid her arms around his neck and kissed him with a decade's worth of passion. Jenky suddenly held her at shoulder's length as if making a positive identification, but then, with the wild eyes of a startled stallion, he kissed her like he did at Dove Creek.

At first, the room was quiet, but then good-natured laughs and wolf whistles rained down upon the scene. Soon Violet and Jenky were alone. They gathered his papers then sat in the corner of the room, holding hands.

Violet thought she might faint from happiness. "Did I surprise you?"

Jenky blew out his breath in a low whistle. "You are the most magnificent surprise any man could hope for." His eyes roamed around her face and her hair. "I see you are wearing your hair down for our kissing session. Shall we begin another?"

The hair again. "No, not yet. And you have to get over my hairstyle, Jenky. It has no secret meaning. I have come to encourage you to propose to me."

He couldn't stop grinning. "What brought this about? I thought you never wanted to see me again."

"I was wrong. Here goes...I kicked out my renter. I found your love letter to me that he had hidden in the tack room and was quoting to me as his own words. I found that despicable, embarrassing, wicked, disgraceful calendar that he had used my photos for...I did not pose like those pictures, Jenky. You have to believe me. He hinted they were for the *National Geographic.*"

Jenky tried to say something, but she held up her hand. "I spent the infamous rent money on new clothes and I intended to buy a bus ticket to come to Denver and charm you into marrying me, but instead, King drove me up here in his loud, giant truck." She held up her hand again. "Don't ask. But on the way, he and I helped a stranger that showed me how precious life is and that more than anything else in the world, I want to spend my life with you." He kissed her hand.

She wasn't ready to start kissing again. "Remember when we were kids and I couldn't go with your family to Denver? Instead of telling me that you were sorry, you gave me a rock. That's how you function. You let rocks do the talking. I do not want another talking rock, Jenky. If you can't tell me something, then write it in a letter and give it to me, face to face. I do want *you*—all day and all night—from now until the angels carry me away."

The enchantment worked. Jenky dropped to both knees right there. "Violet Vera Hendricks, will you be my wife and let me cherish you as the treasure that you are, will you let me love you as no man has ever loved another woman, and will you let me buy you the biggest Sears kit home in your catalogue and build it for you wherever and whenever you want it?"

Violet nodded. "Oh, yeah. With all my heart, but only if I can take a bath while you are shaving. Wait, I didn't mean…" She blew her nose.

"I know—like the Sears page for bath fixtures on your wall. I was thinking of buying ours from Caesar's Deluxe Bath Fixtures. What do you think?"

"Jenky Butler." She covered her eyes. "That calendar was shameful. How dare you look at my face on those bodies."

"You have such a beautiful face. I didn't notice anything else." He was still grinning.

"You don't expect me to believe that for one minute. Is that why you punched him?"

"I had to do something, Vi. I was sure that you were falling for him."

Violet looked straight into his eyes. "It has always been you and only you. As far as the calendar is concerned, I have it in my suitcase to destroy while I am far away from home."

Jenky shrugged. "Good idea, but I have fifty-nine more like it at the house. You'll never find them, either."

"Well, then it looks like I will have to marry you if only to destroy them."

He traced around her lips with his finger. "The first thing I am going to do when we get home is to clear our secret path so we can meet on it for our wedding."

"Oh, Jenky." She sighed and laid her head on his shoulder.

～

On August 23, 1939, Violet walked from her house and Jenky from his. Caesar and Bean stood with them where the paths met along the trickling waters of Dove Creek. No ill wind blew, no crows cawed, and no storm clouds hovered. Violet's wedding gown was from a fancy wedding shop in Denver. She carried her papa's Bible and a bouquet of roses and wildflowers. They exchanged gold bands and said vows before their minister.

After the private service, Mr. and Mrs. Butler hosted the grandest public party that Dolores County had seen since Colorado got its statehood. Tillie Roberts and her sons played their slowest songs first, so Jenky could dance three times in a row with his bride. A buzz was created at the party due to the fact that King of Prussia Lewis had actually gotten a haircut, trimmed his beard, bathed in a real bathtub, and was wearing a suit and tie—the source of which everybody knew.

Everyone had also heard that Violet was giving King her house, complete with plumbing and soon to be wired for electric power. He entertained the attendees with many engaging and especially unique dances and winked at Violet every time.

The newlyweds traveled to Denver for their honeymoon where they strolled through Elitch Gardens and talked about loving one another from afar for almost half of their lives. They toured the Denver Art Museum and discussed names for their children. They held hands at the Colorado premiere showing of *The Wizard of Oz*, and they dined at their elegant hotel, the Brown Palace.

～

In their hotel room, Jenky read aloud an article in the Denver Post about their wedding and also a related rescue on Wolf Creek Pass that took place during a freakish, early summer storm. It was written by a very grateful reporter.

Violet listened to the rhythm of his voice as he read. It was music to her. His tender touch brought joy and comfort she'd never known, and his sweet presence filled her heart with longed-for peace and contentment. Now she knew love. *With all delays and stubbornness behind them, their love would serve as an anchor, fastening them securely against whatever storms washed over their lives. Love conquers everything.* That was the endearing toast that Jenky had made at their wedding and that was the hope that Violet carried always in her heart.

Author's Note

In 1951, my family moved from the Texas Panhandle to Dove Creek, Colorado. Our belongings were pulled along in a wobbly cotton trailer. My parents' first teaching jobs were at the small school there, and I was in the first grade. One of my memories of that time was using the elementary school outhouse. There was one for the boys and another for the girls. I had never seen a multi-holed outhouse before, and modesty kept me away from it as much as possible.

That winter was cold and snowy but oh, so fun. We lived at the bottom of a hill, and sledding was something I had never experienced. The grownups built a bonfire to keep us warm at the top of the hill, while we kids zoomed down the middle of the street on our sleds, and then trudged back up. My family moved back to Texas after that snowy winter, but many Dolores County residents have lived and worked there for generations. They are a hardy bunch.

Small farms like Violet's still exist today. Working any farm is hard labor from dawn to dusk, spring through winter, and much of the family's income depends on weather. Farming families have always been working partners. Before houses were powered by electricity and had indoor plumbing, the adults were exhausted at the end of the day. Whether time was spent sweating behind a plow, at the end of a hoe, or bent over a stove that cooked food for supper as well as heated water for washing and bathing, farm life was not easy.

On May 11, 1935, President Roosevelt signed an executive order establishing the Rural Electrification Administration (REA). The Rural Electrification Act was not passed until 1936, when the lending program was set in motion. It eventually brought electrical power to rural homes, making the future of farm life brighter for everyone.

Coming next...

Waiting for You
BOOK TWO

Raining Love in The Highlands

Sharon McAnear

Kyla Ford has been waiting for love most of her life. She hasn't had a date since the seventh grade, and even then, his mom made him ask her out. She's a successful businesswoman now, and hoping to find happiness in the Highlands of Scotland. But when she falls for Andy Bryce, his old girlfriend and the Highland weather just may steal him away. Kyla has to take charge in ways she's never tried before. Aye, go for love, bonnie Kyla!

Sharon McAnear is the author of eleven books. She lives in Colorado with her husband.

sharonmcanear.com

65245184R00096

Made in the USA
Lexington, KY
05 July 2017